as if fire could hide us

Also by Melanie Rae Thon

NOVELS & STORY COLLECTIONS

Meteors in August

Girls in the Grass

Iona Moon

First, Body

Sweet Hearts

The Voice of the River

In This Light

Silence & Song

CHAPBOOKS

The 7th Man

The Bodies of Birds

FINE ART EDITIONS

Lover

The Good Samaritan Speaks

as if fire could hide us

a love song in three movements

MELANIE RAE THON

TUSCALOOSA

FC2 is an imprint of the University of Alabama Press

Inquiries about reproducing material from this work should be addressed to the University of Alabama Press

Book Design: Publications Unit, Department of English, Illinois State University; Director: Steve Halle, Production Intern: Kamryn Freund
Cover image: *Fire Sky* 2017, © Wendy Thon; courtesy of the artist
Cover design: Lou Robinson
Typeface: Adobe Jenson Pro

Library of Congress Cataloging-in-Publication Data is available from the Library of Congress.

ISBN: 978-1-57366-200-0

E-ISBN: 978-1-57366-902-3

movements

The heart breaks
and breaks
until it breaks open

—from a Sufi prayer

Orelia, in hiding

❖   ❖

I remember birds
or the shadows of birds
hundreds of hearts
trembling through my body

.

.

.

rain rivering my skin
damp earth and sweet decay
piercing cold pellets of hail

.

.

I slept or died

.

.

.

.

and when I returned
stars swirled high
between black branches

.

.

I was not afraid

.

.

.

I did not imagine leaving the forest

2

Orelia, didn't you always love the dark,
the dirt, diving down, staying under,

burying yourself deep in a ditch, leaves
or snow, the ravine, a culvert, digging

a hole in the vacant lot, mud and moss,
so little air, you could die here

Mother at the lab that night. *The night forever in question.*
She calls three times—six, nine, eleven-thirty—*eat your
dinner, go to bed, I'll be home soon.* Orelia does eat: corn-
flakes with chocolate chips and raisins, all soaked in milk,
a soft sweet mash, topped with petals of pansies, petals of
roses, *forbidden flowers*, a deliciousness she becomes, twelve
years old, Orelia Kateri, body in bloom—so she imagines—

In truth she's undergrown, a thin flicker of electricity, stron-
ger than anyone would guess, *Orelia*: the mystery of matter
converting to energy: 4 feet 9 inches tall, 71 pounds, absent
from school 63 days this year—*troublemaker, truant, feral
daughter of delinquent parents*: the father 227 miles from
home, *so many nights gone, so long under*, Nic Kateri: savior, salvager, deep diver dredging up sunken boats, planes
crashed into lakes, flying cars plunged off bridges—

who to blame: numbers now seem important

His one, his only—never can her father bring Orelia to mind
without seeing the other, the twin born shrunken and mum-
mified: no blood in the brain, the lungs, the fingers—*Noelle:*

4

as fire, she breathes, becomes a tiny heap of ash, charred slivers of bone that won't burn: she could be anything now, songs deep in the woods: the owl at night—

coyote, crow, thrush, warbler

He carried the leather pouch of ash three days before scattering her to the waves, a cold November day, wind and rain, the consolation of scrawling birds: *No,* Renae said: *I don't want to know where; I don't want to go with you.* Now, when he dives, Noelle speaks through the arms of sea stars, the green glow of lanternfish, the bodies of ronquils and electric rays, wolf eels, requiem sharks—beautiful and blue, she stuns; she lights his way: eyes huge and wide, she stares; she swims close to kill or save: hungry and afraid, she wants to touch her human father—

Noelle sings, the voice of rain underwater

Please, Renae said, *no name.* She doesn't want to read it on a page or hear it shouted on the playground. Doesn't want Orelia to know—as if she can forget, all that time in the womb, twenty-four weeks—

evolving as we did, fish to human

Renae woke in the night and knew—*a sudden stillness*—
stumbled to the bathroom, flicked the sizzling light on and
off, and again, faster—spun dizzy, stung by electric flares,
waiting for the pulse of light to spark the child's brainstem.
Cell by flickering cell, the mind goes dark, the world quiet. Outside, one bird in the night: the thrill of syncopation
gone: Orelia alone and not alone, deep in her watery cave,
hiding, clinging to her sister—Nic and Renae see them this
way, the next day in the sonogram—

But she does let go, pushes her emaciated sister to the edge
of the womb, thrashes and kicks, bewilders her mother in
the night—

why so strong, why this fury

Terrible now to know the fierce and the dead inside her.
No words to explain. *Take her, please.* But the doctor can't
take one without the other, and Renae says it again, *please*—
mouth wide, eyes popped open—she's been twisting her
hair, pulling hard, wearing scarves to hide the evidence: skin
scratched raw, scalp bare in patches. She leaves shimmering
copper strands tangled in the sink, blood on the pillow, a
language perfect and precise, meant for Nic to find—*please*:
she wants both gone, *outside*, wants to lie on the bed in the
dark, to lie fallow—

In our womb, my sister's heartbeat gone faint and slow, then suddenly absent. Impossible to speak this grief—then or after. I heard the low ripple and hum of my father's voice, the unmistakable music of him entering our bodies—

Cat cry; birdsong; the shades pulled down; the shades opened; my mother's shallow breath; rush of blood and rain on the roof; the slow pulse of her; my fast flutter—*insistent; cruel*: reminding her: two cribs; two slings; two car seats. Terrible to see: that relentless stack of diapers. She tried to stand. She crawled to the bathroom. In the fog of night, alone in this sealed room, wind-borne rain tearing leaves and petals, she wished me into decreation: imagined us, my sister and me, weeks before, spectacularly fetal, days when we might have become any four-limbed creatures:

> *bats or birds*
> *salamanders, turtles*
> *white deer, white mice*
> *two glass frogs*
> *veins & organs*
> *gorgeously visible*

And before this: fish untethered, swimming in the sea inside her. *So small*: fins instead of hands and feet, ever so quick, flickers of tails—

Slanted rays through barely open blinds, luminous dust, galaxies forming: my mother remembers everything alive with light: walls and floor and dust, a pale hand moving through time, water in a glass, the glass shattering—

If she lay very still, if she refused words, if words lost all sense and became music, we too might be undone, my sister and I a cluster of cells resorbed in her, undividing—

Twelve years later and Orelia is gone, so soon will be—

how can he know, why imagine

Orelia's father, 227 miles from Seattle, anchored off the shore of Oregon—he's been down under five times today, taking his turn, searching for the sailboat, believing he might be the one to find a child inside, *skin violet, nerves tremoring,* alive in the sweet torpor of hypothermia, fluttery heart almost but not yet still, breathing slowly, *hushed,* floating face up, a bliss of air trapped above her—

In the last minutes of twilight at the surface, in swirling silt underwater, Nic Kateri risks a final dive into the murky cabin of the sailboat, finds her with his hands, not his eyes: *yes,* where her mother left her, the child curled into herself, lungs full of water, pressed high above the bed in the tightest corner of the berth where *yes, it's true:* there might have been bubbles of air once upon a time, hours earlier—

who to blame, how to measure

9

Even now in fast fading light they might be spared—

if only I stay down with you,
if only we stay under

But *no*—he's been gone too far, too long, nineteen fathoms deep, his delirium a kind of rapture. Hypothermic and almost out of oxygen, the body betrays him, brings the surface of the water so close he sees the last radiant rims of light at the edges of clouds, green and violet—

it's done, it's over

The veil between ocean and air tears: into the hands of his friends he delivers the child—

Silhouettes, merciful strangers: one wrapping the child tight, swaddling her in a tiny blanket, two others lifting him into the boat—so cold he's lost their names, their faces—but their hands, their hands on him, tender as the shadows of birds: these he knows, these he remembers—

Beyond them, the dark coming on and on: *as it does, as it will*: everything, every night, becoming other—someone very kind and quick peeling his second skin, the black suit that protects and doesn't, *murmuring,* guiding him down the stairs—someone long ago and now helping him into thermal underwear—faces so close they might kiss, *as children do, as lovers, as a mother soon to die kisses her only son*—covering him with fleece blankets—

As if he can be warm, as if one day he might again be human—

all, all, and even you can be lost

They wait on the pier—*mother, father*—one dark shape in the dark, void of words, yesterday's crimes swelling inside them: reckless now they know taking a child so small out on a breezy day, *less than thirty pounds*, leaving her alone to sleep in the V-berth below them, not listening to petrels and gulls—watching but not reading their flight, *loving the bruised sky*, trusting the forecast they'd heard that morning, *gentle breeze becoming moderate*, yes, *lovely it was*, white horses leaping out of long waves, the joy of riding them, loving too much their wild beauty, not checking the radio again even as birds cried, *high winds and rain not predicted till dusk*, believing they'd be docked at the marina hours before the weather deteriorated—

ruined in a day

Mother and father failing to envision birds vanishing; a sudden blow from the west; wind surging swiftly toward a gale; white foam streaking across the ocean—now and forever the woman wants to climb below deck; strap the child tight in her tiny pink floatation vest; wants to lie down next to her— *ever, into, float with her*—but already it's too late to leave the man, *alone, in this*—and she chooses to imagine the girl nested between pillows, rocking in a dream, safe in the cabin—

destroyed in a moment

Impossible now to know what it was, *debris or driftwood, a bleached tree tossed by waves cracking the hull*; water filling the bilge; the electric pump kicking on, *too low to hear, too slow to compensate*; water pouring into an open wound— *not sensing, not knowing, the weight of water bringing the boat down*—each believing the jolt they'd felt only the crash of waves, *only water*, outside not in—even now in darkening day, *deep in delusion*, neither father nor mother calling the Coast Guard, keeping faith in their skill—even now in driven rain, the woman working the wheel hard, the man lowering the jib, reefing the mainsail halfway—

all shall be well

The man using the traveler to control the boom—and still the boat so hard to steer; mother and father each without language blaming the other—

Did a word of rage take shape in the man's mind; did he turn to accuse; did he shout this word into the wind—*he'll never know; he can't remember*—only she will recall: the spar whipping in a crosswind, line of the traveler ripping through his hands, the boom striking his head, the father flung across the deck, the unconscious man flying toward the water—

impossible to believe

And now, *ever*, at last she feels it, the boat sinking slowly down, her child unsafe below, the father bobbing in waves, floating fast away from them—impossible to explain how the body thinks, how swiftly adrenaline empties the mind, *blood surging to muscle*, how in this deluge—*epinephrine, cortisol, testosterone, serotonin*—the body makes mysterious choices—

> *white horses break and rise*
>> *rise and shatter*

The woman with her impossible strength finishes what the man started; lowers the mainsail—and now, too late, hears the pump, calls the Coast Guard, activates the locator beacon in the pocket of her vest—

> *thought streaks as foam*
>> *across the ocean*

Even now the woman denies how much water might be in the bilge, refuses to imagine how soon water will break the sole, flood the cabin—

Never in the days and decades to come will she be able to invent a story that explains why the body chooses not to go down, rescue the child first—why it chooses instead to start the engine, circle back, find the father—why in a delirium of dopamine, the body believes saving them all still possible—

whatever word of rage he'd cried
only by wind remembered

A miracle to see him there, buoyed by his red vest, popping up high on white waves, disappearing in the hollows between them—impossible to believe she can get the boat close enough—but she does, *thirty feet*, there is time—

we are close, we are safe now

In her madness, in her love, she tosses the life sling, a yellow horseshoe—unspools its 125 feet of floating rope: so much more than she needs—

If he were conscious, he could swim ten feet, haul himself through waves, grab the rope, pull the sling, slip so easily into it—

but he's gone, down deep
in the dark of himself

She circles him, closer and closer, and the rope begins to spiral: as it should, as he taught her: *the way in is the way out:* a gold labyrinth of rope to save them—

The boat so slow, *mercy or curse*, sluggish with water—she knows everything now, and still serotonin floods the mind, bestows faith in a future—

do not be distracted

Quick and calm, absolutely focused, the woman lifts the boarding ladder over the side of the boat, secures it to its brackets—already she imagines climbing the four steps back into the boat, hoisting her limp husband up and over—

a story to tell, years after

She is telling it to herself now as she leaps in the water, following the line to the sling, swimming the sling toward him—*willing him to wake*—slipping the horseshoe over his head—*and still he refuses*—pulling one arm and then the other up and through the sling—

skin gone white, mouth purple

Now and forever she feels the tug of the rope; sees how low the boat sits in the water—*tilted starboard, sinking faster*—and she knows all in one gasp the choice her body has made is forever and terrible; the adrenaline that once sustained now poisons her—she tries to swim to the boat, *to the child,*

tries to drag the man with her—three strokes, five kicks, all
she has, all she can do now—

impossible to explain

Waves pull her back; the rope tightens: if they stay tethered,
they'll go down with the boat—forever and now and so fast
she pulls the rigging knife from her pocket, cuts the cord:
the body wants what it wants: to be alive—even here, *even
now*, one more moment—

> *all, all can be lost*
> > *the particles of one*
> > > *dissolve into all others*

Childless parents hanging on a single sling, terrified and human, *abandoned*, chopped by waves, swallowing water, *de-
pleted*, small now themselves, lost between blue-gray clouds
and gray-green water—

> *why not go down*
> > *why not stay under*

Weak and wasted, *numb*, the man waking and sleeping, the
woman failing and failing again to dive, *to die*, to sink fast or
far enough—

*Never in the ten thousand nights to come will one dare to ask
the other how it was, why it happened—*

Rescued, they are, childless parents—the emergency locator beacon pulled from the mother's pocket; strobing its light; beaming its radio signal to a satellite circling the earth; the satellite flashing it back again: *time and space, all illusion*: that miraculous message guiding the Coast Guard pilot close enough to see the strobe and yellow sling, a man's red vest, the woman's neon green one—

Flooded with gratitude as they watch the helicopter hovering, small in the vast sky, blades slicing air, a devastation of sound whirling closer—

Shattered as the rope and basket swing free—as the man's bowels unspiral, as the woman's unstrung heart swings out across the water—

Desolated and saved as a swimmer stays in the water with him, as two crew members pull each one alone into the fuselage—

Through all the years, all the evacuated days to come, the man will remember watching the woman as she hung between infinite sky and infinite water, the green ocean going black, the sky rose and gold, radiant turquoise too beautiful to believe along the horizon—never had he loved her more than this, never more despised her—

Now, waiting on the pier, they could not stand, could not be,
could not breathe if not for each other—

> *You, even you can be lost*
> *in a day, in a moment*
> *dissipated, dispersed, void*
> *and without form*
> *the songs of birds if birds*
> *were water, swallows disappearing*
> *into dusk, days of rain*
> *damp earth and sweet decay*
> *your broken body emptied and filled*
> *revelations of light*
> *your flung free sown self*
> *full of light, soon to be*
> *a field of tulips*

Floppy Bear: ears chewed, leg missing: loved too much, washed too often: his stitched eyes never close: his mouth will not open—

At some forever unknown time between her mother's second and third call, Orelia tucks a thin mound of dirty clothes under her blanket, slides the limp body of Floppy Bear into the heap, nestles the battered bear into her pillow—

go to sleep, I'll be home soon

Two flights under Floppy Bear, she feels her way through the clouded maze of the basement, cracks a high window just wide enough for a thin girl to slip through, disappear in the rain, *become the rain*, that way—

So easy it will be to return, *rain back inside*, not wake her mother—

Renae tastes blood and salt, iron, copper—feels with her tongue the insides of her cheeks bitten raw. Doped into sleep, drugged to waken, Orelia's mother sits at the kitchen table with two officers—this dangerously delicate man, this woman with translucent skin, red lips, blue veins pulsing at the temples—

Negligent mother, accused, convicted: impossible as it seems to lift the weight of her body, Renae does rise, feels blood rush from head to legs—she could faint; she could die here—

no, not now, not with them watching

She wills herself across the room, lifts the buzzing arms, uses fumbling hands to close the shades so these two who witness—who wait with piercing patience—won't see her eyes, so the dim light of this day won't touch her face, her hands, her left shoulder—says again and for the third time, what she knows, what she remembers, why she stayed so late at the lab, infusing her aging mice with the plasma of young humans, proving again the bewilderment of transfusion—confirming, *yes*, the blood of one restores the other—

It's nothing the officers want to know—the woman's bright mouth blisters open:

Did you have an argument. Do you know
Your neighbors. Has your daughter run
Away in the past. Is she a good student.
Does she chat online. Does she have a boyfriend.
Where is your husband. A salvager,
You say—

rats, coyotes, gulls, ravens
scavengers everywhere
cleaning the world

The house seems large—

squirrels live in the walls
pigeons roost in the attic

When did he leave town. Have you noticed
Anything missing. Is there cash in the house,
A gun, jewelry. Do you own a dog—

raccoons have torn through the trash

Can we see her bedroom—

A kind of magic: blood collected from human umbilical
cords spun in a centrifuge, gold plasma rising to the top of
the tubes, red cells sinking; the plasma slowly transfused
into Renae's mice—*sacred and transgressive*: so easily the
blood of many enters the body, *becomes the body of another*—infinitely more elegant than parabiosis, that primitive
experiment: even now her fingers remember meticulously
stitching old to young, mouse to mouse, sewing veins together, *flesh of my flesh*, making them one through skin and
vessel—*never in life or death shall you be parted*—

In those last days, she would have sewn herself to her father—*sutured veins, fused my bones to his, stayed in the narrow bed, days or years, bars up to keep us safe, rocked in that cradle till everyone we loved died or forgot us—*

Days from now Renae's miraculous mice will scurry through mazes, memory and muscle mysteriously rejuvenated, bones strengthened, metabolisms boosted—in a life imagined and now riven, Renae sees herself at the lab with Orelia, watching the mice together, timing their runs through twists and turns ever more tangled—

Bodies quickened, minds awakened, wild hearts beating seven hundred times a minute—

Better for Orelia to be here than at school: *delinquent*, yes, mother and daughter, *delirious truants*, witnesses to resurrection—

Never will Renae say how it was, lying there with him, only the mute twilight tender enough to touch them, the light dissipating, each molecule of air violet and visible—their bodies now not bodies at all, nothing more than places where dusk gathered close, and the air in those places darkened—thirteen years gone, and even now she dreams him alive, heart scarred, lungs weakened by pneumonia, every organ failing, her father so close and always leaving—

In the dreams, no sister, no mother—she is always alone
with him. He is falling down the stairs, falling in the water;
sliding down a cliff; breaking on the rocks below her—

She swallows coffee hot enough to hurt the esophagus—
tells the officers once more: *home at midnight, just after*—so
she says, and who now can contradict her: the blind bear,
the rain, the mice at the lab, her missing child—

No breath, the house too quiet. She remembers a slant of light
from the hallway falling on Orelia in bed: *so I believed, so I
imagined*—7:44 this morning before she discovered Floppy
Bear, eyes stitched to the face, two black *x*'s—

And yes, Orelia's cell phone missing too—so it's true what
the thin man says: *she could have been anywhere when you
called*—true what he doesn't say: *the ravine, a culvert*—

He's not afraid, this hunger artist, shoulders narrow enough
to drop down a crevasse in search of a child: *heart of my
heart, I hear you:* faithful enough to blow dirt from her eyes,
breathe into her—

From the room on the second floor, from the unmade bed,
from the tossed heap of dirty clothes that smell of mud and
leaves, Floppy Bear whispers: *a hole dug in the dirt, a dog's
house*—

She's not answering now, battery dead or phone tossed—the
small girl stashed in a trunk or trapped under floorboards:
Orelia, three blocks from home, buried in trash, drowned in

a dumpster: the child unconscious, arms and legs torn by brambles, down deep in the jungle, drifting beyond dream, hiding in a nest of rags, a fog-filled bed under the freeway where the sound of rushing cars is the sound of the ocean, the sound her father hears in his death of sleep, Nic Kateri, still cold in a floating bed, his motel room submerged, broken free from the ship, a berth underwater—

Orelia, not even you know the minute, the hour—but yes, you do remember riding in the rain, the green mountain bike borrowed from your neighbor's garage—you remember the brilliant line of light under the door—an opening, an invitation: you love him—Tom, Tom Ariely—this forgetful man who watches over but never speaks to you, who tempts, who fails to flip the lock, who wants to free you—you love his wife, Joanna—bones of the skull, the ribs, the clavicles—Joanna starved to bliss, living on light, living on flowers—day after day Joanna kneeling in the garden, dry hair the color of bones, the color of ashes—how can you explain—love comes as it comes: when she stands, dark dirt falling from her knees breaks you open—Joanna: you sing her name in the night, a prayer of gratitude: impatiens, lilac, calendula, clover—Joanna: so mercifully she forgets lavender, lovage, snapdragon, violet—the petals you pluck, her unfathomable losses—

Irradiation, evacuation—Joanna scooped out, cut, sutured, infused with toxins to kill and save her—all her beautiful children unborn—

Nasturtium, Basil, Zinnia, William

25

She can starve herself to rapture, *yes*, Joanna, high and light
and full of God, but every loss remains, *Lily*, *Angelica*, incar-
nate within her—

It's true, she knows them—senses them in breast and brain,
stuttering thyroid—the unborn imperishably alive in lungs
and spleen—skin, liver. Their pluripotent cells crossed from
placenta to blood, found their way to bone and cartilage—
they vanished and remained, recreating themselves through
her body—

lips to kiss, arms to hold us

Joanna: not one, but many: in the heart, her children's cells
become muscle to repair damage—in the hippocampus,
the unborn spark genes to express themselves and excite
neurons—her ecstatic children fuse their immaculate bodies to neural networks—even now they are whispering to
her, laughing now with one another: *Calendula, Impatiens,
Zinnia, Violet*: she breathes them in, all together, then one
alone: so sweet he is, *Sweet William*—

William: who spilled into her blood, a murmuration of cells,
finding his way to the valves of the heart where forever now
she hears him opening and closing: the inexorable surge of
him, their blood a torrent—

William: who offered his sweet self even as his body stayed
his, connected by the cord, feeding from her, 129 days in the
cradle of the pelvis—*William*: perfect feet, perfect fingers—
William: the last to come, cells from every sibling inside

him: *yes, it's true*: and his father through them to him—*and back to his mother*: pulsing red to the veins of Joanna's hands, blue to the heart, an endless loop of memory—*William*: the weight of a flicker, a bird who can eat the berries of poison oak and poison ivy—thistle seeds, moths, snails—

Glorious, gliding in the garden: red nape, black whisker—flickering, *yes*: gold light flashing in the wings, coral fan of tail feathers—

here I am: the heart of the heart of a bird fluttering inside you

In the garden, love is dirt and rain: through every wet blossoming Joanna hears children singing—

Orelia, quiet as stone you lie,
not wanting, not waiting: safe
between raised roots, a fizz
of nerves, sparks in the brain,
blood darkening dark earth: breath
by breath leaving the body:
you hear Noelle, your sister, born
and unborn, the voice of rain, underwater

Love comes as rain and fog, the cries of crows, their soft laughter

Naked in dark water
my father's body falls
into another cosmos

galaxies of phosphorescent
fish whorling above & below
between legs & fingers

he knows the exact force
of their love: open
mouths; curious mercy

my father swallows bio-
luminescent beings
he swallows water

the belly glows, blue &
green, a globe of light

God inside the man
as he is in the ocean

vast, my father, scattering
stardust, too weak to move

his arms, too numb
to make lost legs flutter

he is not afraid; he has
no will, no strength, no
desire now to gather
a self & leave the ocean

Father, what is it in us makes us
love this death, this sleep
        sinking down, becoming other

Here I am: in the fog, in the rain, flowing under the West
Seattle Bridge—

raccoons run
on the roof
even now
do you hear them

How can I explain: a line of light, the door unlocked, the
door open—and *there* in the bright garage the green bike
flecked silver, polished for children unborn: waiting for Lily,
Zinnia, Angelica—*now and evermore*—waiting for Violet
to live, to fly—waiting for William to ride away into—

Father, she stood at the window, *Joanna,* wished for me to
take the bike, make the glitter of its green frame disappear—wished for Tom to stop oiling the chain, adjusting
the spokes—she wanted him to stop pedaling the bike
down and up the hill, testing the gears—her tall husband
ridiculous on the child's bike—a man mystified by desire:
as if he believes even now the sixty-three-year-old woman
without a womb might bring forth a child—

Joanna, I saw you at the window: thin gauze of your night-gown lucent in the glow of the kitchen light far behind: I knew every porous bone of you: your body radiantly exposed, transfigured in X-ray—

Stung; electrified—shimmering in the rain—the sparks of me turn brilliant and scatter—

> *Joanna, who, if not you, can understand*
> *the desire to be gone, to go dark, to be other*

Hungry, yes, it's true, missing less than an hour and starved already—twelve thousand seven hundred seventy-six homeless humans in Seattle tonight, *any night*, so I've been told, so I'll learn after—

> *who can count, who imagines*

Dread of Life Mission—I misread the sign in Pioneer Square—

Everywhere I ride: battered cars riddled with rust; bright tents; tiny houses—shacks built of scrap in the beds of trucks—*everywhere*: driftwood on the beach; cardboard boxes; tarps strung through saplings under freeways—free, *yes*, the ones who sleep in beds of rags under trees in the park—free in alleys and parking lots, drainage pipes, jungles—*this is my house, my crib, my cave, my mother*—wet

sleeping bags tossed in the weeds safer than any shelter—
every night cities within the city appear—*reservations, sov-*
ereign nations: we make our own laws, reap our own justice—

All night and everywhere, shivering shadows—*do I dream*
you: children wearing black garbage bags over black hoodies: they sleep standing up, tilt unsafe in doorways—

Everywhere, fires flare: the disappeared flicker into being,
divine or dead: junk from the child dump, glittering eyes
and grinning mouths—*rabbits, goats, ringtails, coyotes*—
crumpled paper ablaze in the skulls of animals—

> *rats rule the earth*
> *gulls circle landfills*

Orelia's father lies paralyzed in sleep: cord of the motel phone pulled from the wall, cell phone on mute: he wants no one to wake him—here, deep in his blue-black cosmos, he forgets the child rocking in a boat at the bottom of the ocean. He is nothing more or less than this sea that surrounds, this sea that fills him. Drowned and quiet, he loves every phosphorescent pattern of light, every transient being moving through and out of him—

He will not remember mistaking cold for peace, opening the window wide, the mind becoming air; fog, the skin; waves, the body—

8:58 a.m.: Orelia's mother calls the motel desk clerk, enlists this unknown boy to wake her husband—

Pummeled, drilled with vibration—his body a grief of sound, mind irrupting—someone pounding, unlocking, entering— something speaking—

A word arrives: *no*: in his own voice, and another voice answers, words collide, erasing each other—the one outside his body thrusts a phone into his hand—

No: Nic Kateri breaks back into himself; hears bones splinter—

And the voice through the phone insists on a language even the bruised brain can comprehend: *she's gone, Nic—Orelia— missing—*

He is suddenly, terribly awake, alive, and the boy who has brought him back from the ocean braces against the wall, afraid of the man who spins too fast—shoving feet into boots, zipping a green flannel jacket over blue thermal underwear, stuffing clothes in a bag, the phone in his pocket—whirling once around the room before leaping through a portal of light, the open doorway—

> *fog giving way to fog and still*
> *too much, too soon, this brilliance*

The mercy of no words in the car, no news, no music: Orelia's father cranks the heat high, drives fast, stops only for gas, two extra-large black coffees, three chocolate-filled chocolate doughnuts—hunger a hole; the body returned; the mind vacant—

Not yet ten, and already fifty-seven misleading leads: *Coeur d'Alene, Reno, Missoula*—floating face down in a river or sleeping safe in a tangle of thorns—

> *unscratched, unscathed, Orelia untorn*
> *quick as a wren, flying into here*

Father, I would like to tell you I am following the tracks of wolves, walking to Canada—

Here is the truth of it: in the alley behind Western Avenue, I saw a man with four prostheses, metal claws for hands, digging through trash, hoping for fish bones to pick clean, chicken wings, chicken hearts, cold fries soaked in ketchup. *Never*, I told me. But hours later I see a child standing beside herself, choking down three bites of dry bagel, swallowing with gratitude dark dregs, some stranger's bitter coffee—

Too weak to ride home, too tired, too dizzy—light coming on in the rain, Orelia could call her mother, *confess*, be done with it—but the cell phone is gone, *lost*, lifted or slipped from her hip pocket—some shadow of herself has cracked the code, is calling her parents, hanging up, calling again, *breathing*—calling her sister: *a curse, a threat*: both waiting—calling the brother she loves: *I see you at your window; I'm here; so close; so cold; come find me*—

All we want now is to lie down, *sleep*, be dry enough to stop shivering—

Father, everything you love can be lost; you know it's possible:
after your mother died—lungs pocked, liver glowing—your fa-
ther died, naked in the shower; then your cousin; and the dog—
yes, even Viktor—and finally Zizi, your sister: one leg gone
at the thigh, osteomyelitis, infection deep in the bone, bacteria
spilling into blood, sepsis, body and brain awash in poison: no
blood, no bone, no rain streaking the window, nothing you have
to give: no birdsong, no river of love can save her—

With rain falling fast, the road Orelia's father drives is a river—red, orange, green, silver cars skimming the surface—

Blue flames   *boats on fire*   Mother

Father, Sister   *bodies incinerated*   fragments

Of crushed bone   *pulverized to sand*   copper, lead

Arsenic   *one child*   and then another

What remains of remains   strontium, lithium

Manganese, cobalt   the missing, the dead

The soon to be gone   luciform in the rain

All the beloved   *dead*   blazing past you

And the forest, and the rain—*why are the people in cars not afraid*—sword ferns high and wide enough to hide a nest of femurs and skulls, ribs, vertebrae—

> *why do they not know*
> *why are they not weeping*

And the trees, so green, *too green*, saturated by rain—why
are the children not terrified of trees, skins slick with rain,
strangled by vines or covered with mosses—

why do they not see

Even fallen logs decay, disappear, become dirt, wash away,
leave roots of trees they feed raised, hollows so deep fish
might swim here—

Ever green, ever growing, fourteen feet of rain a year, the
trees here never dormant: spruce and hemlock hundreds of
feet high, maples making fog, a forest making weather—

*Father, I am not afraid, even as the copper skins of madronas
peel away to expose wet green flesh beneath them—*

Unceasing roar, horns flaring: he is already here, home, the
traffic of Seattle brutal—

He pilots the car through this annihilation—

in breaking light
  into a sky vast & muted, pink
    & lavender, the white gull
      flies high, catching light
        becoming light, a point
          of light between clouds vanishing

Father, with photophores bright as eyes, lost children watch over us

1:22 p.m.: my father delivers the disheveled wreck of himself to my mother: *sounds rising from their chests but no words*: they stand forehead to forehead, unable to move closer. Cold in the house, wind blowing through, as if somewhere windows cracked, as if all through the house windows broken—

Hour thirteen: time now measured by light, where it falls, what it touches: the glass, the floor, the face, the table. The clock jumps or stills: my mother makes toast, brews pale green tea to soak it. My father climbs upstairs and down, looking for fractured glass, finding the window in the basement open: *cold, yes*: but he leaves it this way—for rain or raccoons, *in case*, if ever—

8:29: Orelia Kateri sighted 242 times: *Spokane, Tetonia, Aberdeen, Wallace*: Her parents following her through streets and alleys, more than five hours now, tracking her from one end of Seattle to the other: Orelia seen roaming downtown with a pack of children—and later, with night rising up—*between trees, behind houses*—Orelia just one of a thousand drifting through neighborhoods: *here we are*: rooting through compost, eating skinned skins and fermented fruit—*and here*: foraging in gardens, pulling up flowers and vegetables, feeding on leaves, loving rhizomes—

We climb trees to fall out of them—

why do we not break
why are we not crying

We lean over bridges, *wailing into the wind*, daring one another to leap, howling our way from bliss to obliteration—

In dumpsters, in gullies, in garbage, we find missing parts: things once immaculate and now ruined: a miniature violin: wood warped by rain, neck snapped, strings dangling—bones in a sack of skin: thirteen ribs, twenty-seven vertebrae: the orange cat a relic of herself: tail chopped off, tail too tempting: the once-waving striped tail pierced by a hook, hanging behind clean clothes in a closet in a house where a child sleeps, protected by his mother—

The boy with black dreadlocks jumps into a green bin, digs and digs, and there it is: a baby grand pink piano, fourteen of thirty keys gone or silent, and still the boy plays perfectly: *a hundred kisses deep and more*: the boy sings to her: *first loved, first lost*: baby sister—

From dirt and debris, *trash tossed down a ravine*, we unbury a doll with blue eyes—blind now, all head and no hair, stunned glass eyes rolling in their sockets—

Beatific Talking Betty, *beloved Betty*, do you dread life— where is your arm, your hand—one would be enough—*is that your body*—if a missing child pulls the string on your back, will the naked head start speaking—

41

Hungry, hungry, hungry—even Saint Betty starves—no more words of grace, no beatitudes, no blessings—

Whoosh of cars, falling water: in the park over the freeway, lost in a maze of sound, the cellist hides between slabs of concrete, pulling psalms from strings, hearing prayers through rivers—

She might be an angel if not for the blue and black wing of a butterfly covering the right side of her face, thorns circling her neck, the tattooed viper coiling down her left arm, green lit with gold, opening its mouth wide above the elbow—

> *she'll play all night*
> *sleep is death & no music*

We are not afraid—

Two paramedics rip wide the shirt of a dead man: one pumps the chest, cracking ribs, breaking the sternum: one jabs a needle hard against the thigh, delivers a dose of epinephrine potent enough to kill if the heart of the heart of the man had not so long ago failed him—

> *let the dead be dead*
> *let the blood stay quiet*

And still the cello sings, the vibrations of its body pulsing with the one who plays: *valves opening, blood surging*: its range the range of human voices: *hers and ours, the paramedics', the dead man's*: strings humming into hollow wood— *ribs and back, hard maple*—heart, lung, open mouth—belly of spruce and long spine: *the song of one becoming other*—

The man stays where he is—*undearly departed*—splayed on concrete, *dread of life*, refusing to rise: *why stumble out of the cave to hear again sisters weeping*—   .

Heaven now would be home, hot chocolate, the warm kitchen—me and the dead man and the cellist and two dozen lost children—all of us and Betty restored to herself but blissfully quiet—*and more, and ever*—a man with hooks for hands; two tired paramedics—*a multitude pouring into the house*—so many I believe the house is a heart, broken open—

The container of powdered chocolate and quart of milk keep refilling themselves; the tiny tin of lavender shortbread has no bottom, no end, no empty—

> *Father, you've come home*
> *you sleep upstairs*
> *you spoon my mother*

An emaciated man and flock of animals wait in the yard— as if I or anyone might refuse entry—

Long white beard, white hair tangled: he brings a Bengal cat with green eyes and spots like roses—beguiling, yes, but no more beloved by him than the ones tossed from cars, thrown from bridges—*denied, disowned, scrapped, neglected*: cats with torn ears and gouged eyes: *frozen and revived*: skins hot with sores; hair matted—*a bite, a look, a scratch will kill you—*

He's been fasting fifteen days: *to be kind*, he says: *to be hollow—*

One red roan cow follows him: *ivory-splattered rust, dark eyes, long lashes*: she alone has escaped the slaughterhouse, battered her way out to walk this earth, gaze at clouds, graze on grasses—

Thirty-nine million cows condemned to die every year—
One hundred and six thousand, eight hundred and forty-nine today—
Four thousand four, one hundred and fifty-two just now, this hour—

Three gray langurs have unlocked their cage at the zoo: *missing*, the posters say: *black hands and ears, black feet, black faces—all less than two feet tall*: do not be deceived: *silky hair and sad eyes; delicate limbs; spectacular tails—*

Who else could have emancipated seven bears—*blue, black, white, spectacled*—irresponsible rebels: who other than they had reason to release thirteen flying foxes, five Siberian reindeer, one sleek civet whose musk will daze and destroy you—

Who besides a delinquent monkey would dare to liberate the eight-foot-long Komodo dragon: *sixty serrated teeth; claws sharper than knife blades*—

Four llamas with shaved necks reel down the hill outside the house—they've spent their lives guarding goats or sheep, kept from others of their kind so that they might choose to protect the children of strangers. Now, together, intoxicated with the scent of roses and azaleas, haunted by visions of green plateaus, they want to go home—

that snow, those mountains

We would walk with them if we were not so tired—

Father, we would rather die than see the clouded leopard tracked and tranquilized, transported, leashed for walks, displayed on television—

The man blesses all who pass: camel, boa, flamingo, zebra—

nothing tame, no one wild

The coyote is here and not here—she's evolved, become nocturnal—she'll eat your trash, but prefers to snatch mice and voles—frogs; geese; fish; rabbits—she loves raspberries and fallen apples—she's the ghost girl befriending wolfhound and terrier—shepherd, spaniel, basenji, poodle—she eats their food, drinks their water—

She circles just beyond the length of their chains; runs away with their bones; chokes them with frenzy—

She leaps and howls with the little papillon at your window, but loves most your Irish setter—desires as her own the feathery red flume of him, that waving wing of red tail— she chooses for herself, for ones unborn, this quivery, quick, superfluous beauty—

And so it is the fleet coyote carries silky red children into the world—

She has hurt; she has hunger—a family not so different from yours, a heart cracked by loss, memories of bodies close in the den: four brothers, one sister—parents who brought food; nipped and taught; nursed and protected—

How many now among the dead: shot; torched; drowned; poisoned—

Father, we want to wash the man, *bless him*, anoint him with basins of water—

Homeless before he was born and even he can't say how old: forty-two, ninety-seven—

two thousand and thirty-three

A thief spared, forbidden to close his eyes, condemned to witness—

for you alone: this annunciation

Who but he can count—who remembers:

bluebirds caught in a blizzard
feet frozen to wires

vireos flying into refracted skies
glass & clouds
concrete & steel

red-eyed, yellow-throated
voices forever still

warblers, babblers
shrikes, greenlets

whole flocks of iridescent
starlings sucked
into the engines of airplanes

who but he hears
their gorgeous
glossolalia

thrushes, orioles, larks, flickers

each one speaking
directly to God
lungs full of fumes
wings flared in fire

Who but he imagines bowels and brains, lungs extending
the full length and breadth of their impossible bodies—
thousands, millions: so many lungs opening into the spaces
of hollow bones, absorbing oxygen, exhaling or inhaling—

Who will tell of their huge hearts, six times the size of human hearts in proportion to their flying bodies—

       vultures, swans, swallows, sparrows

Who sees the utter catastrophes of them; who gathers feet
and splintered keels; who washes them clean, after—

       far away, wind moves through grass
       a prayer, a vast prairie of wind

       here is the last word:
       a whirr of wind
       through white turbines

Father, the voice you hear now is not the voice you remember—

If I return from this, *from ever*, it will not be as one you know:
I have been scoured out; I am transparent—

Mother, here is the truth of it: I survived only one night on the street. I met many starved men, many animals. I saw birds, broken or dead. A pigeon rocking on a sill fell in front of me—

I confess: I skidded in the rain; flew from the bike; scraped palms and knees; bled from my nose and forehead. It hurt to ride. I ditched the bike by a dumpster near the market; left it for some other child to find; imagined her riding home; using the key dangling from a long chain around her neck to slip inside; waking in her own bed; hearing her parents' voices—

I balanced Tom Ariely's loss with this child's ever—

Each choice creates a future: a spectrum of unbidden possibilities—

Before dawn, before you found Floppy Bear and knew I was missing, I saw the blistered blue truck parked in an alley off Western Ave: arctic blue, the color of ice: glinting in the rain; pocked with rust; paint peeling into other blues: sky, ocean, aqua, cobalt—

Twelve thousand seven hundred seventy-six
homeless humans, this night, every night, this city

Tents, tarps, dumpsters, doorways—shopping carts draped
with blankets—nests of rags, stick houses: from these possibilities, I chose the blue truck; the man slumped in the
passenger seat; this future—

David Zaer: fifty-two years old, sleeping in his truck because he'd missed the ferry: I loved every bone of him: huge
hands, long fingers—long arms and long legs—sharp vertebrae, winged scapulae: broken: many times, many places:
tibia, ilium, eye socket, clavicle—

I knew the ruin of him: something sweet: a brother long
lost, forty years older, fractured and familiar—I accepted
every possibility of us so swiftly becoming—

He'd pulled a tarp over the long blue bed, stretched it tight,
cords hooked through grommets. Easy enough to release
one corner; easy to climb up and under. In the bed, I found
three flat boxes cushioned with blankets, all labeled *glass*,
all stamped *fragile*. Tucked behind them, in the far left corner, he'd left another tarp wrapped around a black trash bag
stuffed with a dry sleeping bag—

as if he knew I would come, as if he wanted to save me

He did save me: I stripped wet clothes—ripped jeans,
hooded sweatshirt—slipped down deep in the sleeping bag

under the tarp and was gone, *unconscious*, unknown to my waking self, *untouchable*—

Did I dream or remember: hundreds of fish pulled from the water—

pithed through the brain or cut through the gills, bleeding

—the deck slippery with blood, me falling—

And later: slashing the throat of a cow, the cow blinking, moaning and gurgling—the black cow with a white face watching me saw off her legs, seeing herself open—

And beyond: learning to snip DNA, altering the genomes of pigs, holding the babies—loving the quick flurry of them: elf ears pink inside, pink wet noses—

Pitting apricots; pitting cherries—feeding the pigs their favorite foods: grapes, snow peas, kale, spinach—cutting pears and apples from their cores; chopping cucumbers—offering strawberries from my own hands—helping them grow strong, keeping my marvelously reinvented pigs joyful long enough to stun their brains, put them under—

Harvesting beating hearts, holding their hearts in my hands, holding pink lungs, long bowels, red kidneys—stitching their organs inside baboons: *xenotransplantation*, such a magical word—hoping one day to transplant the organs of pigs to the bodies of humans—

Mother, if you feed the puréed body of one flatworm to another, the living worm remembers an electric shock delivered long ago to the one inside it—

I do not forgive us for the mice we made part human—

We loved them, yes, but not enough. You injected ketamine or sodium pentobarbital. I held them. I wanted to feel their lives move beyond their bodies; wanted to know them as they passed between one thing and another—

I cradled our mice after you ever so skillfully performed, *as we say,* cervical dislocation. What we mean is: I watched you apply quick, resolute pressure to the neck, separating the spinal cord from the brain—

Approved, we say. *Ethically acceptable*—

How many minutes does a cow, a fish, a flatworm stay sensible to pain—

How long can the body of a mouse receive love, language, scent, sorrow—

Cloud, nerve, murmuration, cosmos—who knows where memory resides—

> *My memory now leaks into the earth*
> *and air, flows as water flows, seeps*
> *down deep through dirt, travels*
> *across miles of mycelium*
> *My memory now becomes the forest*

You told me: *no, stay home today*—you said I might just once go to school—

I hid under the plastic cover of the cargo space in your little hatchback. I was there, in the lab, with you; I held the sleeping mice; I insisted. I saw insides turned out—

Splayed on their backs, the mice looked like tiny humans—

Mother, I am witness; victim; accomplice. I saw you slice bowels and brains into the finest slivers—esophagi, spleens, pancreata, muscles. We examined every part of our mice under the microscope: vivid molecules stained pink and blue, green, violet—each cell illuminating multiverses of possibilities—

And they were young again, it's true, transformed by the plasma of humans. Eviscerated, spliced, stained: every particle of their bodies served as proof, irrefutable evidence—

In the ravine I found a coyote snared in a steel trap: she'd lived long enough to starve: I felt the bite of the trap break my own leg—

as if, as now, as ever

I sat beside her till dusk. No one to tell. I did not want to go home. I wanted to walk all night with her ghost beside me—

I chose the blue truck and woke rocking on the ferry. *Vashon, Canada, Lopez Island*: I lifted the tarp just once, trying to see where we might be going. Some mother must have noticed the slash of thin face looking out, eyes glittering. She must have wondered why, written the license plate number on the back of her hand, taken pleasure in this, a tattoo, not indelible—

In this way, the misaligned man standing on the deck in the cold salt wind became known as David Zaer, Person of Interest—

It's true: I fell in the rain; I bled. I left skin, hair, blood—the elegant double helix of me—in a sleeping bag under a tarp in a stranger's truck—

David: seven years sober, but tonight the delirium will return—tonight: *fever, confusion.* The officers appeared in late afternoon: *not to accuse*: only to question. Two men wearing white gloves took the tarp and sleeping bag, the black trash bag. *With your permission.* A tow truck came. The blue truck impounded. He was not under arrest. *Stay close to home*, the younger officer said. The boy was ridiculously pale, fuzz of white hair, *a white cat*, skin bleached, eyes yellow—

How far could he go without the truck? If he started now, he might walk to the rainforest, be lost by daybreak—

His sister, his real sister, offers aspirin, cold water. *To bring your temperature down,* she says. She helps him hold the glass, asks again: *Did you know? Did you see her?* He is no longer sure. *Never, no.* That's what he said this afternoon. Tonight he says: *I don't remember—*

Tonight he tells Marion: *The tarp; I saw; unhooked at one corner.*

It is like the other time, seven years ago, and now, again, that dazzling light, the child zipping out between cars on a skateboard. The child moving from shadow into light. Edges blurred. David Zaer not drunk but hungover. Slow to respond. The feet heavy. *And the light.* The boy flying into the street—*too quick, so agile*—leaping into the air to spin. The light blasting through him; the body gone; becoming light—as if the truck might pass through; *light into light;* never touch him—

Both to blame. David unbruised. The child broken. Right radius. Left fibula. Concussion. He was home before dark, resting. He did not remember the truck, the man kneeling in the street beside him. His head hurt. *Yes,* he remembered sirens, being lifted up. *And the light.* That part was beautiful. He was tired of talking. His arm hurt. His leg. He asked his parents what happened. They told him again. They called the doctor. *Not unusual,* she said. *To forget, a mercy—*

By morning words slurred. He said they looked weird—
furry. He laughed and then he felt sick. He forgot he was
hurt. He tried to stand. His father caught him. He vomited.
Spewed something green on his mother. It tasted horrible—

His mother tried to keep him awake in the car. He didn't
want to be awake. He wanted the birds to stop. A crisis of
birds in his skull. *Not pretty.* His head felt huge, his brain
swollen—

Something clear and pink leaked from his right ear. His
mother said this. She sounded very calm. His father drove
faster—

We almost lost you. That's what they said, his parents, when
he wanted another skateboard. When they caught him riding his bike without a helmet. When they locked the bike
in a storage unit for a month. As if he couldn't walk to the
skate park. As if a friend wouldn't let him borrow a board.
As if he couldn't steal. Who cared about the bike. Locked
up. Imprisoned—

never mind, whatever

The helmet was neon green, *radioactive,* aerodynamic with
twenty-two vents, LED lights, detachable visor. His parents
bought him gloves to match: black and green—black shoes
with green soles and green laces—

They thought they could tempt him—

The child they brought home from the hospital was not the boy they remembered. They wanted someone to blame. Someone to be held forever accountable. *David Zaer.* Not legally drunk. Not criminally culpable. They won their civil suit. One hundred and seventy-five thousand in damages. Compensation. As if this or any amount would ever be enough. As if anything could bring the boy back, *Sweet Dalton*, the one dreamed; a child imagined. The man was forbidden to come within five hundred feet of their son. This felt good. Illusory satisfaction—

They did not calculate how it would feel to have the money invested, to watch numbers on the screen multiply in the years after—how it would feel to have four hundred ninety-two thousand when the boy was gone: on the street or dead; living in a driftwood house; floating out to sea with the tide; swimming back as something else; unrecognizable—

Seven years and here he was, spun backward. Something had happened to him. *Because of him.* He couldn't explain it. He wanted to die again. He did not say this to Marion. She who cosigned the loan to pay the damages, who offered her house, *this house*, as collateral. She who loved him back to life. *My garden.* White stones, white tulips. His sister who planted and hoped. Fed and waited—

He wanted to drive off Snoqualmie Pass, fly into a sea of stars, spin into a night so dark stars stormed and swirled— he wanted to get it right, not be rescued, *not be repaired*, not return, this time—

David Zaer worked four hours the day I chose him. Replaced three shattered windows. Charged Mikal Whitaker only the cost of the glass. Mikal was the daughter of Marion's best friend from high school. *Louisa, Lou, Lulu.* Dark hair and green eyes. Pale skin spattered with freckles. Limbs too long. Clumsy. *Intractable desire.* He never told anyone. Something about her laugh, *Lulu,* or the way she and Marion laughed together. Two sparrows inventing music. Sometimes two coyotes, howling. Girls wild with things they could not explain—

For him, *with him,* no one, ever—not the wife who divorced, not the daughters who made excuses. They preferred the stepfather: unscarred, *unaccused:* a civil engineer, clean hands, perfectly symmetrical—

Louisa gone last August. Cancer spotting the left lung and then the spine. Pain transported her. *Please,* she said to Marion, *my daughters. And Jude. He's not a bad boy—not really.* Jude, Louisa's grandson. She wanted Marion to watch out for them—Mikal and Jude and Polina—*if you can; if they'll let you—*

Jude was the breaker of windows. Rocks thrown from outside. For the irruption of glass. Glass breaking in. Glass embedded in carpet—

Because walking barefoot should hurt. Because a hole is not a stutter—

Because Mikal, the mother, *his mother*, will not ask why—

Because she knows. Dishes broken in the sink. Mugs cracked in the cupboard—

Because his grandmother and five months later Aunt Polina—*glioblastoma*. Quick. Polina's mother spared; Louisa dead before she knew her daughter's diagnosis—

Because Polina here, *with them*, those last months. She and her sister hadn't spoken since the memorial. Jude's mother let her come. Endured Polina's obscenities. Who knew there were so many. *Profane:* everything could be—

A chair, a window, a bed. *It won't be long,* Lina said—

Polina: smoking in her room; windows open to the rain; bald head exposed; withered body. *Lovely Lina:* green-eyed like their mother—

Eyes clouded now. Sunken in their sockets. Pink nightgown hanging loose. Letting Jude see how it was, what was happening. Three boyfriends even now. Only one returned. *Ray.* Eighteen years older than Polina and just paroled—

Stray dog in the rain. I look sweet to him—

Ray restored a dirt bike; pawned his brother's gun to buy new tires with yellow spoke skins, deep treads. Taught Jude to ride. The riding felt like flying, *something good*, a gift that would last. He gave the boy a real leather holster and a black water pistol. *For killing rain*, Ray said—

The wet holster smelled of the animal it had been—

Polina showed him how to drive the silver truck: so smooth, humming as she shifted gears—infinitely patient as he jolted down the road, stalled, started. And again—*and over*—

She pressed the key to the truck into Jude's hand: *ours*, she said. She meant the secret of teaching him to drive while her sister was at work. She meant the hot shower together: because Polina so cold and too weak to stand alone after driving—

Ray in prison again by December. Seventeen dollars and change. Holding up a convenience store with a toy gun—

Brains of a vole, digging in—

Carton of cigarettes. Liter of Coke. Never now coming back—

explosions of glass

Because the pigeon, the squirrel, the rat dead—

The BB gun and he never meant, didn't intend—

Because tiny heart and terrible feet—

Because 117 bones and the head of a chicken burned in the trash—

Because later, in the road: the spotted fawn, ravens, the gray cat—

Mother, I escaped in the rain. Left the one-legged bear and a heap of dirty clothes in the bed to deceive you—

Yes, if you insist on words, the line of light beneath the door of the garage tempted me. I did not borrow: I stole the mountain bike. Trespassed without regret or fear against my neighbor—

I chose the blue truck, the misaligned man, David Zaer, our future together, the possibilities of him. I believed my own lies; intended to climb out as I had climbed in; imagined finding my way home to confess. Scraped and cold as I was, I trusted you and Tom Ariely to forgive—

I did not climb out. I had fallen in love with the man, the warm sleeping bag, cedar and pine, the smell of him. He delivered me to Mikal and Jude's house, far from the three other houses I could see, the edge of a forest: leaves of the maples wider than a child's face; bark black and shining—ferns five feet tall, insistently green—hemlock and fir; spruce, cedar—

I waited—let the man move deep into the house, the boy's small bedroom—

I gathered torn jeans, black shoes, soaked hoodie—slipped inside and down steep stairs into the quiet dark of the basement—

We smelled the dead woman everywhere—

My clothes spun in the dryer while he vacuumed broken glass from the carpet, shards grinding through the hose, the boy's fractured music—

Then the man was gone, and I climbed into the body of the house; drank milk from the carton; used the bathroom—

In Polina's room, I found her blue fleece bathrobe in the chair by the window where she sat to smoke. I took her into my lungs. I was not afraid. I fell asleep wrapped in her robe under her bed—

Father, you would like it here, this dark,
this ever, this deeper into. Birds.

Speaking slowly. Long spaces
between songs. Years, miles.

We might be dead here. No
longer contained, skin sacks

expendable. After the rain,
water dripping from needles
and leaves falls into us.

We are mud and moss; fathoms of
rhizomes; mice climbing over;
microbes seeping out and into.

Stars so dense they blur:
we cannot open our eyes;
stars inside and all around;
we do not know how we see them—

The boy home hours before his mother—dusk spilling into the house and his was the dirty hand covering my mouth, his the jittering leg over me—

He sensed me, a living thing: pulse and vibration, the pressure of air against his face, something new and inexplicable: not the torn-up, gray shred of cat he fed at the windowsill, not Polina—I was the scent of someone else, not his mother, intermingling—

Bowel to throat, an animal cry rising through me—

the quick hand over the mouth

the leg pinning me

the body close

the hand dirty

the body hot

the boy electric

don't be afraid

he could spark the house

burn it down

torch us

Twilight: Orelia Kateri officially missing twenty-one hours. The rain has stopped: clouds open at the horizon over the water to reveal a strip of pale rose below faint gold. Since midafternoon, her parents have been following leads, showing her photograph to kids hanging out in Pioneer Square, giving them cigarettes, coffee, five-dollar bills—*please, a few seconds of your time*—distributing photocopies to families living in tents north of the city; revealing her height, her weight; describing thin face and hazel eyes to anyone who will open the flap of a tent and listen—scrambling under the freeway where hundreds of humans stoke fires deep in the jungle—offering up their only child again and again; exposing her ever more strange and startling ghost—*dark hair, loose or coiled, just past the sharp blades of her shoulders—bangs she cuts herself, deliberately jagged—*

Orelia Kateri: the disarray of absence—

She proliferates: all these images of her, all these missing children drifting through the world—

A man parked in a rusted gold Mustang tells them he saw her three days ago. *In the ravine*. A tiny person, blinking fast. For fifty dollars or six oxycodone, he'll take them to the place he watched her burned and buried—

If you want to die, go out in the rain and show images of anyone you love to strangers—

Maybe it was true: maybe he had seen a girl murdered— *three days, three years, three hours*—who can know how time travels through another human mind, what a man might remember or dream, sleeping in this car with cracked windows, living here, in this alley—

Home, haunted by visions of tarps and trees and cars on fire, Orelia's father takes a shower—hot then cold—water pulsing hard and harder—

Nothing changes—

He doesn't know where to go. The nightlight glows green at the top of the stairs. Some kind of answer. She's there, on the bed, the child's bed, in the dark bedroom. He lies down on the other side, dirty clothes and a bear with stitched eyes between them. Red rhododendron blossoms flutter in the wind, the tree tall enough to see through the window. Beyond this, a maple. Night coming up from the ground. Dark leaves and red blossoms turn ever darker—

Tell me, Renae says. She wants him to describe the girl drowned in the boat, her parents, what they did when they saw the white blanket, the child inside, weirdly blue, curiously bloated—

He does not know. Drifting in and out of sleep, he rocked below deck, still close to hypothermia—

He invents what she wants to hear: *First the mother then the father held her—*

Does not say how it felt, her small body in his arms, rising to the surface, the nothingness of her weight in water, wishing they could stay under, losing her to his friends, seeing her body disappear, swaddled—

Then and now imagining the days to come, knowing the future—

    house
       stairs
          mother
             father

    separate rooms
    a hallway of footsteps

    milk & beer in the fridge
    fruit gone soft
    half a pizza

    a dozen eggs misplaced
    exploded in the freezer

Years or days, how long do I lie between roots,

hidden by ferns and fallen trees, known by ants

and worms, mosquitoes, spiders. A doe and her fawn

come close. Nothing is afraid. Black rats

and jumping mice—fox, vole, skunk, marten—

Small fast feet move over me.

Scattered light finds its way between limbs

and leaves; touches briefly the forest floor.

Light is God.

I would move my hand into the light if I were able.

We ate half a box of Chocolate Chex, finished the milk, spilled sugar. I lay down in the boy's bed. He promised to keep me safe, a secret from his mother—

He did not try to touch; did not cover my mouth; did not use one leg to pin me. I woke many times; walked out into the night; circled the yard and returned; risked waking the mother. I sat in Polina's soft chair, opened the window. So easily I might have fled, run to another house, pounded on the door, accused the boy. He stayed awake, eyes open, waiting for me to decide; come back to his bed or betray him—

In the morning, I heard them in the kitchen, the mother's voice rising. No milk for her coffee. Cream gone sour. Why didn't he send a text. *Unreliable, inconsiderate.* Black coffee hurt her throat; her stomach—

Whipped cream in a can; ice cream in the freezer—*I'll make cinnamon toast.* The boy's suggestions enraged her—

A slap, smack of her open hand fast and hard across his face—

Everyone's breath held—

He could slam her to the wall, defuse her—

I'm sorry. You're sweet. I'm crazy—

Yes, they both were—

The porcupine, the cat, Polina—

Fires in the trash can—

Louisa—

Small cuts on his feet—

Broken glass embedded in carpet—

The road, the rain, the skunk, the ravens—

Mother, I confess: I stayed with the boy, watched him quickly and too easily trust me—

Because small and thin as he is, he outnumbers me by three years, twenty-eight pounds, six inches—not like the girls at school, soccer players with strong thighs—big girls catching him under the bleachers—arms to choke, legs to trip him: three laughing girls and why? He can't remember—only this: one pinning his wrists; one his ankles; the sweet candy breath of the blonde girl on top, the weight of her crushing him—one rib cracked and then another—he could die in the dirt, slants of light under the bleachers blinding him—

Because he can't imagine how a girl like me could hurt him.
Because there's so little we need to say, and when he speaks,
he does not stutter—

Orelia Kateri: she's the wounded animal under your porch, rain streaking glass, a heap of bloody rags in your basement. As the night intensifies, she's a wasted dog crawling out of the ravine to forage scraps from your mulch bin. She's sleeping in a cardboard box in the weeds in the jungle; burning in a box three other children set on fire. She's a girl up in smoke; whirling in the wind; falling down as ashes—

Dreams, lies, confabulations: so many people wanting to help, deluding themselves, wishing they'd seen her—

Specks and splatters of blood in a sleeping bag and the bed of a blue truck not enough to prove harm, not enough to make a Person of Interest a suspect—

Orelia missing forty-one hours, and now two black Dobermans dig in Joanna Ariely's garden, *canine officers*, such delight, smelling me there, finding me among nasturtium and violet—

The dogs forcing Joanna to confess: *Yes, the flowers and the bike; I wanted the bike gone; I saw her.* All night and all day she'd told no one. Hurt, bewildered, and now sorry, Tom understands at last: the garden, the grief, *all these years*, what he's done to her—

Eight hundred twenty-one children missing tonight in the state of Washington. *Children*: meaning eight hundred twenty-one human beings under the age of eighteen, including fifty-two not yet ten. Numbers that do not account for those abandoned in grocery stores, motel rooms, campgrounds—children deliberately discarded hundreds of miles from home—*dumped, deserted*—left drugged and drowsy off trails deep in the woods or high in the mountains. *Saved or not saved*. Numbers that leave no space for those who stayed out one night and then another, who disappeared in the ravine, the river, the snow, the jungle—ones whose families somehow failed to mention clothes in the trash, sheets crumpled—

a man with a white beard
sits at the water's edge washing
the bones of fish and birds
slaughtered cows
coyotes snared in traps
mice cats deer children

You who are afraid of children remember a dark thing stepping from an alley in the Square at dusk, moving into the glow of a streetlight, becoming human, dressed in torn jeans, black hoodie—she asked for change, a cigarette, coffee—you tasted sweat and breath, yours and hers—the adrenaline rush: bitter, metallic. You gave her three dollars and she laughed. All the way home, she floated in the rearview

mirror. You locked the gate, the garage, the car—you bolted the door from garage to hallway. But later, that smell,
in your house; filthy clothes in a pile in the bathroom; her
sunken shape, bones dissolved: the bog girl, stained from
peat, hair shaved to stubble—one more murdered child, five
hundred years gone, leather of her skin miraculously pre-
served by cold salt air, humic acid—

Later, the clothes gone, the floor clean—*no one, nothing*—
but the memory of her will not leave you—

Here is the truth of it: the boy and I rode his bike along a
dirt road deep into the forest: bodies hot, then chilled, all vibration. The river roared, roiling blue with silt washed from
the glacier, surging with ice and fallen trees, torn limbs, broken branches—

> *river of the dead*
> *skunk   raccoon   flying squirrel*
> *a coyote too starved to swim*
> *white mink   red fox*
> *spotted owl   tiny black bear*

In the forest, Jude Whitaker gave me his water pistol. *To
shoot the rain*, he said. *Or kill me—*

Three emancipated dogs found us: one black and golden
red, *fearless*, blue eyes shockingly pale. One lean and tall:

75

long hair, long legs, white lit with blonde, eyes dark and sad, waving her flume of ragged tail. The third skittish and quick, smaller than the others, huge ears, golden eyes, half coyote—

The blue-eyed one caught water in her mouth, circled me till I stood still, coming closer and closer, smelling me, sprinting away when I tried to touch her—

She sensed everywhere I'd been, everything now and gone and still to come—

On the way home, the boy who broke windows trusted me to carry the gun, wear the holster—

> rut and stone; engine revving—
> the clutch through hips and spines;
> bodies one; ribs shifting—

Mother, I did not dare to imagine you looking for me, riding the ferry to the Peninsula, driving from Kingston to Port Angeles, baring my face, revealing your failure—asking shopkeepers and store managers to tape me in windows, knowing I might be ripped in half the next morning, crumpled and tossed in the trash, burned out back or crushed in a landfill—*disfigured, destroyed*—your child disappearing again, ever and into—

Father, I did not hear the cries of petrels and gulls; did not see another girl's parents holding their drowned child; did

not yet know how cold you must have been as you broke
the surface—

Later we lay on the boy's bed, watching the shadows of
birds and the shadows of leaves flutter through curtains—

We were still, the way children are still at the bottom of
the ocean. Drifting through the quiet of late afternoon, I
did imagine: *Mother, Father,* both of you home now—*no
lights, no heat*—the bear, the bed, the rhododendron too
red in the rain—rain on the roof, in the street, down the
gutters—dark leaves, wet grass, the impossibly wide crown
of the maple—on the bed, *my bed,* you heard rain dripping
from leaves long after the rain stopped falling—

All this and still I failed to imagine the police at the door,
a different pair: two men, detectives, both tall, dark in their
dark uniforms, filling the doorway—*just a few more questions, please*—entering the house, not wiping their feet, the
force of the air they moved moving through you—

> Has your daughter been ill. Does she take
> Medication. Do friends come in the house—
> Repairmen; neighbors—

> > *roots strangling pipes*
> > *toilet overflowing*

> Did you know, have you seen
> A basement window cracked open—

rain spilling in

Will you take us down.
Shall we close the window—

   splatter of blood
   on the basement floor
   rat or raccoon, something
   dead, someone hiding

And yes, if you don't mind,
If it's no trouble, can we look
Upstairs, one more time,
The bedrooms, *please*, also the attic—

   window broken, pigeons fluttering

I asked the boy for his cell phone, and he refused—

From the core of me to every capillary, hot blood rushing—

In my mouth, the taste of copper—

I said, *okay*. I said, *no worries*—

He was in the kitchen making grilled cheese with peanut
butter sandwiches when I slipped down the hall into the
bathroom, locked the door, climbed out the window—

In my mind, in some impossible future, I was home, asleep
in my bed, body buzzing—Mother lying close, careful not

to touch, not to hurt, not to wake me—*and you*: afraid to close your eyes, remembering Noelle, cold wind and ash, my sister's body incinerated and crushed to dust, floating out on the waves, sinking in the ocean—

And the other one: *Sweet Father*, your body rocking, feeling even now the exact shape of the child in your arms as you kicked to the surface—

Awake, *afraid*, you sit all night in the chair beside me—

Eight hundred twenty-one children known to be gone, said to be missing—among them Dalton Trase, a boy hit by a truck one bright day, riding his skateboard. A child transmuted, one of thousands who can no longer and never again endure living with his parents—

Orelia, you leave your blood in the sleeping bag in a man's blue truck, on Polina's chair, under her bed—blood on the basement floor, in the boy's sheets—blood smeared on his black boots— blood down the throat of the drain—blood washed and washed from his dirty hands—

> *who will collect the blood*
> > *who will measure the blood lost*
> > > *from one particular child's missing body*

The night he spun off Snoqualmie Pass, David Zaer lost three pints in the truck, fifty-five in the hospital, after. *Not as much as some.* Doctor or custodian, a low voice, the edge of consciousness—and his sister's voice: *That's not possible—*

But it was possible. Saved, transfused, he woke with the blood of strangers flowing through him. *Welcome home*, the nurse said. Who did she mean and how many—

He didn't want to be. Lights off, unbelted, utterly and forever sober, he'd flown into an ocean of stars—

a bright cloud of unknowing

Why was he still here, and why so many to save him. Never to be pardoned: he was the one to blame for Dalton Trase, the boy dead or gone wild—

Seventeen surgeries, not recovered—

Brother, I know you. I too have broken ribs, collapsed lung, winged scapulae—

we cannot, will not
ever speak of it: all ravish

& ravage, roaring back, raging
into the harrowed hungering
mess of the body, bones
snapped, muscles wasted
left lung full of blood & mucous
the right a womb for swarming
microbes: unbeloved, indolent
we are infected by language
bones too shattered to fuse
titanium plates, screws
to hold them
truck destroyed; human
salvaged; the face scrapped
brain swelled; brain
rattled; two ribs removed
to make brow and cheeks
repair sockets; the jaw
wired shut; skin from
the buttocks & thighs
stitched to the face
wounds closed
the face, the mouth, the neck
swollen—and now a hole
in the throat, a tube, an airway
you cannot speak
you do not wish to

Your sister brought you home. The tube in the throat gone.
You lay in bed, unremembering. Therapists came, taught

you to walk and speak, lift the spoon to your mouth, lift the weights from the floor, hold the tools. Marion opened the window wide so you could not not hear falling snow, budding leaves, blooming camellias—so you could not evade birdsong, rain, dogs at night, cats, coyotes—

She fed you macaroni with butter and warm milk, fresh blueberries, puréed soup, vanilla ice cream. *Anything you want—any day you want it.* She bought you a baseball cap dyed with the red clay of the desert, a bandana to protect scars from the sun, hide your stitched face, so that they and you might heal—

One day she brought you into the garden. She'd been doing your work every day: planting tomatoes and tarragon, cauliflower, lettuce. *Marion*: speaking to ones underground, waiting for shoots to break through bulbs, rise and blossom—

Now here you are, alive, sustained, delivered into the early light of this day to see a circle of white tulips beginning to give way to red at the center—

Weeks later, only crimson—

White gulls from the sea, white stones gathered at the beach, a white rim of tulips growing wider until five scarlet blooms remain at the center: if you wonder why you survived, the world offers these answers—

Orelia, how far did you think you could run before the boy sped
out on the dirt bike to find you. Why did you not imagine the
finch falling from a tree, a disintegration of crows, the porcupine
dead, the gray cat torn open—

The Glock BB gun loaded
He never meant, didn't intend

But there I was, running
Across a field toward the trees

Tempting him to chase
To hunt, to site, to shoot me

A steel BB through the eye
Or throat so easily can kill you

I could have stopped and turned
Spoken in a child's voice, disarmed him

The double blast
Of the gun surprised us

One hit to the back of the thigh
One to the shoulder; nerves buzzing
Stumbling; seeing only a blur

Of trees, crawling toward them
Rising up at the edge of the trees

The boy bringing me down; the boy
On my back, knee to the spine

Twice I tried to rise; twice the boy
Leaped; brought me down harder

Brother, lover, imperfect stranger, I confess: it is not the boy,
not the knee crushing vertebrae, not the wounds of the gun
that keep me down: it is the stone, the patient stone waiting
all these years, the stone my head strikes that in its quiet
way quiets me—

I was not afraid

.

.

.

I remember my body limp
the boy dragging me into the forest

.

.

.

the songs of birds far away

.

.

.

short riffs

.

.

.

time and space expanding between them

who to blame, how to measure

the boy, the gun, the stone, the field
the girl who rode away in the rain
the man who left the garage door open

cancer of the lung & spine
glioblastoma, quick departures

a water pistol to kill rain
the BB gun to shoot squirrels

splinters of glass, broken windows
chicken hearts burned in the trash
lungs, bones, bowels, livers

the shadows of birds & leaves
fluttering curtains

the boy's father forever unnamed
forever uncertain—one of four
at the grocery store
down the road
long dead, in prison

three laughing girls under the bleachers
cracked ribs, bruised eye
gasping to breathe
telling no one

the girl stealing the bike
the girl eating flowers
mother at the lab late
father underwater

a sky gone green, clouds violet
parents leaving their child below deck
streaks of foam across the water

Joanna waiting to tell
Dobermans digging

a misaligned man
a boy on a skateboard

the girl choosing the blue truck
the smell of the man in the sleeping bag
loving the man, riding the ferry

the mother seventeen years old
pretending the boy could not be
wishing him gone, before & after

the girl slipping into the house
falling asleep under Polina's bed
the smell of smoke
Polina's fleece, Polina's pillow

letting the boy trust, a night & a day
staying with him
riding his bike, shooting his pistol

the neighbor who left the Glock
in a drawer unlocked
in a house unguarded

the pit bull who loved the boy
who licked his hands
who tried to dance on his hind legs
the dog who let the boy take BBs & gun
graham crackers & chocolate milk
everything & all
exactly what he wanted

Twilight again, clouds opening, the man dizzy with light, a glow of coral light filling the kitchen. His sister asks if he ate today, if he's hungry. He's not; he can't remember. The girl gone more than forty-three hours. The blue truck in the drive washed clean, run through the car wash twice, bleach splashed in the bed and washed again—and the sleeping bag too, washed three times, spun dry—when he pulled it out, the zipper burned him—

After the ferry, David Zaer drove to Port Angeles—stopped for gas, coffee—then the house for the Shop Vac before driving to Mikal Whitaker's to replace the windows. Nothing more to tell: No longer useful to the police, no longer interesting. Orelia Kateri could have left him in Port Angeles—or climbed out of the truck after the woman saw a child on the ferry; she might have walked off in Kingston or hidden in the bathroom; taken the ride back to Edmonds; found another truck; a bed full of furniture where a small girl could nest unseen under a desk, a chair, a table—

Vancouver, Walla Walla, Butte, Boise—

She might be back in Seattle by now, dead or not dead, *disappeared*, one among thousands, all the uncountables—

The boy burns his clothes in the trash, hides
under Polina's bed, wearing Polina's robe, head
on Polina's pillow. He sees Polina's eyes open
wide, the last day, unseeing—remembers the gloved
hands of the hospice nurse delivering bliss, delivering morphine—*Polina's breathing so slow, heartbeat
fading*—his face near her face and still impossible
to perceive where Polina crossed over—

The liberated dogs have come to lie close, keep the child
warm, save her. She knows them by shape and smell, each
particular rhythm. Fearless, calm, half coyote. She knows
the consolation of long legs, feathery ears, waving tails. Eyes
swollen shut, but she senses them watching: sees deep in
her throbbing brain their eyes and the eyes of owls and the
light of stars all around her—

The boy under the bed
Denying what he's done
What he's dreaming
A girl in the forest
Eyes bruised, blue, violet
Pupil of the right eye huge
Swallowing light, not seeing
So still, so quiet, blood spilling
From the wound on her forehead
Limbs twisted, eyes red

Where they should be white
The girl bleeding out, bleeding into
Dead or not dead, so soon she will be

Quiet as stone you lie,

a body now for other beings: blooming

out, blossoming into—your hair

lines their nests; your blood sustains them—

nitrogen, phosphorous, potassium, iron—

your cells enter the mycorrhizal mind—

giving up, giving over—a child unborn

feeding stars, feeding microbes

And the light, the morning light falling on the child's bed,
the bear, the heap of clothes, the parents—making a pattern
on the wall, a mirror, a window—

Beneath them, in the kitchen, the refrigerator door opening, water running—the child home; the child hungry; they
dare not look at each other; dare not think it—

impossible, intolerable, another day, blue
sky between clouds, white birds,
green leaves, this world

I was not afraid until I heard the voices of children

Their hands delivered me to pain, the fear of pain, the body

I knew the pressure of each breath

The quick coyote howled and chased them

Muddy footprints through the house, filthy clothes, late for dinner—another twenty dollars gone from her wallet—little thieves, compulsive liars—the children swear to God they found a body in the forest, human, dead or not dead, bleeding from the skull, joints twisted, all purple—

Why should the mother believe anything these two tell her—

It's their father's fault, working the border, appearing as a talking head on the computer, telling them stories, what he's found in the desert: human beings burst open, bodies so toxic even the vultures refuse to eat them—a rattlesnake choking on a horned lizard—open rib cage of a bighorn sheep, head gone, hacked off by hunters—

He's a liar too, tells them he rides a horse at night, a mustang he's rescued—

She threatens to turn him off, but walks outside and down the road, smokes three cigarettes, gives him another twenty minutes to invent a version of a self to give his children—

> *The dark again but no stars,*
> *fog low and close as skin,*
> *fog inside and out, blue silt,*
> *roiling river, fallen trees*
> *and torn limbs, the body gone,*
> *the mind unspooled—*

The mother sees me on the night news, flash of a photograph, another child disappeared, *good God*, one more missing, seventy-one hours, hope of finding her alive diminishing—a bad girl, out in the rain, out the window, riding a stolen mountain bike all night, traces of skin and blood found in a truck on the Peninsula, a number to call if you think you've seen her—*here I am*: black and white: dark hair, light eyes: a little thing—*boy or girl*—she wouldn't know if the suddenly serious reporter hadn't told her—

Only now does she believe her children. If not so much wine, if not that second Vicodin, if the brain not fizzing, she might have gone to their rooms, awakened them, brought them into the glare of the kitchen and asked them to tell it again, *where and what*, whispered, *sorry sorry sorry*—

Bats send songs too high to hear: music reverberating bone to blood and through the belly, revealing bodies so much the same as hers she sees a self above the self, flying with them—

She can't fly, can't spread her arms wide, can't move by will even one finger. Their fugues expose exactly where and how badly broken: four ribs cracked; ischium, ilium, sacrum fractured—left tibia at the knee; right radius between wrist and elbow—

Where scarlet blossoms open in the brain, music turns violet blue, deep and brilliant—

she is not afraid

.

.

.

she feels the spin of the earth, and the earth's rotation

.

.

.

no matter how cold, it is possible now to be ever colder

Father, here I am: very still, very quiet: a body of broken birds: bones snapped, feathers swirling—

Here: stars we can't see, black holes and the cosmos beyond them, consciousness above and below, trees speaking to trees, webs of mycelium, breath entering fog, birds flying through, worms crawling under—

Here I am: a doe coming close as the heart slows, the blood cools—here: three dogs watching over me, God entering time through this body, God breaking me down to my elemental being—

God recreating his broken self, ever and over—

Nine more hours gone before the mother wakes curled in the chair—neck stiff, brain drumming: *something terrible*: a child's body opened, animals scattering bones, ravens feasting—

Lines converge: a blue truck, broken windows, and now two children saying they've found a body, *a child*, less than three miles from the Whitaker house—

David Zaer interesting again, *a Person of Interest*, and Jude Whitaker too, important to the inquiry: because he might know, might have seen something—a weird kid, stuttering, wearing a woman's blue bathrobe—and the mother, Mikal, watching the two policewomen who have come to the door, welcomed themselves into the house to question the boy who will not sit still, who stands perched on one leg and then the other, tilting, pretending he might fall in the living room—

Maybe he found the body too; maybe he saw a man with a scarred face coming out of the forest; maybe he lay still in the grass or hid in the trees, afraid of the man, afraid to tell anyone, especially his mother—so the tiny woman suggests while the tall one nods, taking notes, and the two in this way invent their spectacular tale—

And the mother is saying, *no, not David*—remembering the fire in the trash can, the dirt bike scrubbed clean, boots polished, the boy under the bed and now Polina's robe over his underwear and nothing else, and the boy refusing to sleep in his own room, the boy in the night walking room to room

and out into the yard and barefoot down the road, the boy
she can't stop, Jude coming home, feet torn, body shivering—and the boy is stuttering, stuck on the word *I*—until
finally he spits it out, the terrible impossible preposterous
truth, a story he still can't believe: *I shhh—sh—shot her—*

Jude, into the unbearable world of words, we are delivered—

A woman's flat voice breaks apart through the speaker of the phone on the table, telling the parents yes, another lead, a body of some kind, possibly a child, and yes, maybe their daughter, incredibly alive—*dangerous to hope, dangerous to believe the stories of children*—and please, stay where you are—whoever it is, she'll be flown to Harborview—

Hours later, in the hospital, the parents will recognize muddy clothes: black sneakers with red laces, torn jeans, black hoodie—

But will not recognize the face, the body swelled blue and green and violet, the wine-dark port-stained red of this child's legs, hematocrit so low her blood leaks from veins into tissue—and the mother says, *I need to smell her*—and who would dare to deny such a thing, and the mother does smell, and she knows, despite dirt and damage, yes, *Orelia*, she's certain—and the father signs the papers, anything you need to do, *yes*, transfusion, *yes*, a hole in the skull to drain the blood, to unswell, to save her, and *yes*, titanium and screws and the bones of ones not alive, *and yes, please*, a tube in the chest wall to remove air compressing the lung—*whatever you find, whatever is necessary*—and how can anyone say these words, and how can anyone survive, and how can this in a child be possible—

And so you will be human again, human and many—

The boy in a room
with a woman
red hair, pale skin
not quite young
a soft voice, no
makeup, too kind

a trickster

shown a photograph
a body, some swollen
thing gone green, gone

purple—do you know
do you remember
did you shoot
did you do this

alone, in a cell
wearing paper clothes
on suicide watch

no, not possible
telling yourself
not her, and the gun
the BBs, bad luck
who can believe

they hit—too far
away to hurt
she only staggered

you flung yourself on her
that part is true, all
you wanted was to make
her stop, bring her home
make it all the same
eat the sandwiches, lie
on the bed, make it better

and the rock, why
there in that exact
place, all this time
flat and quiet, and why
was she so still

even then your wild
heart, your hope
she must be
pretending

you lifted one arm
and let it drop, and
it did drop, and her
hand hit the earth hard

you thought she was dead

you never meant to
hurt, you love, you
didn't intend to drag
and leave her

who scratched these walls
and why are you
scratching, why bleeding
on these walls, and why
pounding your head

and why if they're
watching don't they
come now to keep
you from hurting

The girl ten, the little brother eight, leading the way into the forest, afraid now, running ahead of the rescuers, uncertain of what they saw and if it was breathing—the child they touched might be gone now, dissolved, stolen—

In its place, they might find a dog snared in a trap, torn open—

You four who follow come with a board to stabilize my spine, three breathing bags, two disposable resuscitators, a camera to document the scene, tourniquets, splints, tape, bandages, a silver blanket. Alive or not alive, whatever half human thing you find in the forest you intend to strap tight to the board and wrap safe as an astronaut—

You bring epinephrine, morphine, oxygen—lorazepam, dextrose, saline, verapamil. You intend to restore, repair, revive, save me—

You come with your unspeakables—

Ever and now, you feel a stranger's strange aortic valve opening and closing in your heart, keeping blood through your resurrected body flowing—

You bear dreams and visions: a calf you saved from a flooded wash; a woman you didn't—a motherless bear; a lead-poisoned eagle—

You come with two who died, their clear corneas stitched to your eyes focusing light so that you might see a boy under ice: blue eyes, blue skin: a child watching as you chipped toward him—

You carry your self-obliterated sister, the weightlessness of her in you, the shape of her shadow, elongated or crushed small, your sister at every hour—

You enter me as warm waves triggering nerves, opening channels from nose to brain—*too hot, too soon*—six human flames: you blaze red and orange at your cores: gold to green to blue at the edges. Through wet grass and into the shade of trees, you walk with the eyes of hawks and owls watching—

The hammering of your hearts could kill me—

I remember birds, the beginning—even now with your hearts so close, I might choose to leave, might vanish between limbs and leaves, might fly with them—

You come, speaking the word *please* into the whatever of me, understanding all these years too late your extinguished sister's grief, the absolute *no* of no thought—

You calm your breath; bones singing—

Sixteen years old and she found the perfect explanation for pain—

Your father's pistol in the mouth, fragments of bone, face gone, mind exploded—

The door bolted shut and you pounding hard, but no answer, going outside in the snow—no shoes, no jacket—battering the glass, breaking the window, lowering yourself into the room, cutting your hands, your feet, your face, bleeding into her blood, knowing at last your sister's secret—

I am afraid for you, how it will be tonight, remembering me, after—

The snow, the cold, no pain now, the sky coming apart, snow falling into your sister's bedroom—

Your hunger for me is God hunger—

And your father, a torment to himself, *unforgiven*, forty-eight years old and gone—his swollen heart a reckoning: dark energy tearing him apart; lungs shrunken and stiff, honeycombed, clotted with dead bees; the brain a black hole, pulling you and your mother and all the stars and all the light that ever was into the dark matter of memory—

Never even now in any language can you change this—

Never—no matter how many you deliver back to their broken, frozen, heart-stunned bodies—can you save yourself with a different story—

I terrify: the children watch the rescuers touching this creature; stabilizing the neck, the head; photographing the body, the scene, the forest; injecting; bagging nose and mouth; pumping oxygen; tying tourniquets; splinting; bandaging; rolling me to my side; fingering the vertebrae; sliding the board under; lowering me onto it—strapping chest and hips, above the knee, above the ankle—securing a block on each side of the head; strapping the chin; strapping the forehead; covering what remains of me in a silver blanket—

You come to deliver me into the harrowed ruin of the body—

So tender but not ever tenderly enough you lift and carry me, and we move from the shadows of trees into the blaze of the field where he is waiting for me, my destroyed and salvaged, broken brother—

David, you who have returned from ever to now, only you know how not to touch, not to hope too hard, not to hurt, not to wish for anything—

You stand in the tall grass, quiet, swaying as if blown by wind, waiting to see if my face is exposed or veiled, watching four saviors lift me into the helicopter. The children who do not know you know the place where you stand is the only safe place in the field or the forest and they run to you and one leans against each leg and lightly with your huge, exquisitely unhealed hands, you might dare to touch—

But do not touch them—

And the dogs with their sunstruck eyes come to the edge of the forest, reveal themselves to you and the children, wait with you as the helicopter whirrs and rises—

And the mother is smelling her child's skin and the father is signing the papers and the girl is tested and transfused— made whole, made many—scanned, x-rayed, illuminated, shot through with waves of sound—and no one can believe, and the girl is put under, paralyzed, plunged into forgetfulness so that surgeons can drill and drain, set bones, nail and screw titanium plates, transfuse again, save her—

I glow, I tremble, alive, unfathomable—I breathe now from a tube down my throat connected to a ventilator—

Doctors come to my narrow bed with their interns and residents, describing the devastation of me, blood loss and broken bones: radius, ilium, skull, tibia—elucidating the wonder of cadaver bone, the lightness of titanium—

They must be miracle workers, these surgeons—what other explanation can there be for my impossible survival—

Deep in a coma, *yes*, medically induced while my brain unswells, while neurologists wait to access the degree of damage. Impaired, I must be, but for the moment rendered perfectly insensible to pain, so they say, and who am I to contradict them—

I cannot speak or lift my hands to sign, cannot arrest them with a word: *listen*: the tube scrapes the trachea—every breath hurts the core: torn muscles of the chest, bruised spleen, collapsed lung, cracked ribs, fractured pelvis—*please*: the cuff on the arm measuring the precariously unstable pressure of my blood makes another bruise—why do you not know waves of vibrating air crash into the smallest bones of the ear—stirring waves as they whirl deep into the coil of the cochlea, shimmering through cilia, charging molecules—why do you not perceive sparks in your own brains—*electricity, patterns*—words as light passing one mind to another—

Insensible, insensate, so you say—

Listen: the smell of antiseptic stings the brain; your bodies full of microbes whelm me. I am not asleep: air touches neurons high in the nasal cavities, delivering memory and fear—the particular emanations of you—directly to the cortex—

You think you are safe: this is where your own brains open to the world—

I remember the limbs paralyzed, the face smothered—blades cutting through skin and flesh, gloved hands probing inside, plates and screws, piercing sutures—

Do not imagine I will forget this conversation, your scent, your syntax, your pheromones, your scrubbed clean hands moving the air as you speak, your hands in blistering light glowing above me—

The nurse suctioning my tracheostomy tube says, *I read about you in the paper, you're famous—you should be dead and you're not dead—you're here with me and it's night—do you know this—*

Swahili, Zulu, Kikuyu: her voice an ode to joy, an excitation, some mysterious Bantu fusion transfigured through English. If she said I was going to die—if she said, *I come to wash you,* I would—without dissent, without equivocation—joyfully into ever give myself to the rapture of her music—

Yes, a story: the news at five, the paper tossed on the stoop in the morning—

Missing Child Found Alive

Orelia Kateri: a miracle, a lesson, a tale to terrify wayward children and derelict parents—a declamation designed to teach and traumatize unbelievers with the harrowing misadventures of runaways, truants, thieves, liars—a mystery to thrill them with the decimating misfortunes that shall in due time inevitably befall negligent mothers, delinquent fathers—

In the stories others tell, you will not see my mother lying with her father, the mute twilight touching them as he moved across the frontier, as he left her—

Now she lies on a hospital bed pulled close to mine and we know ourselves this way: scoured of words, our bodies not bodies at all, nothing more than the place where the molecules of air become more dense, a deeper violet—

No one will tell you how many nights my father and mother lay on the narrow bed not sleeping, dirty clothes and a floppy one-legged bear between them—

No one counts how many images of me they sent fluttering through the world—

Those who would cast stones fail to imagine a girl no longer delinquent, a person never again required to go to school, one whose parents take turns staying home with her, teaching her what they know, bringing her back into her broken body, touching only the borders of her mysterious mind, walking her down and up the hall and months later the stairs, then through the house and around the park and finally along the water as she encounters again and for the first time this fractured world—a girl whose parents love without expectation to understand—who receive with gratitude this being who has been given back, knowing she cannot tell them what she is becoming now, how she began to evolve again, reconceived in the forest—

In the story, there are four saviors, two brave children, seven brilliant surgeons, 592 leads leading nowhere, one disturbingly disfigured innocent suspect, nurses no one counts, persistent detectives, the disconsolate mother of a not yet named desperate boy locked in detention—

Joanna Ariely appears, self-starved, *withholding evidence*, but without mention of irradiation or evacuation—*no Basil,*

Zinnia, Lily, Violet—no troubling sensations: no image of Joanna scooped out, infused with poisons to destroy and save her—

No flickers glide through the garden, no bird wings flutter inside you—

In the story, you will find no tattooed cellist, no paramedics pumping the chest of a dead man, no defiantly silent doll, glass eyes rolling in their sockets—

Missing from the story are the children wearing black garbage bags over black hoodies—*glittering eyes, mouths open*—discarded children sparking back to life, scraps and twigs set ablaze, *brief flares*, flames in the skulls of bobcats and bears, sheep, llamas—

You will not be invited to imagine the disappeared, thousands of children pouring into the house—so many we believe the house is a heart, broken open—

Red rhododendron blossoms in the wind; beyond them, a maple—

You will not find filthy clothes in a pile in the bathroom, no bones dissolved, no bog girl revived and once again murdered—

On the nightly news, you will not hear the words *xenotransplantation, parabiosis, osteomyelitis, glioblastoma*—

In the newspaper there is no space for stars—

No galaxies, no cosmos, no black holes, no dark energy pulling us apart—no supernovas, no infinite expansion into—

You will be given no time for contemplation, no openings of white between paragraphs to enter the borderlands where you and not-you dissipate—

In the story that is not my story, there are no white mice—bodies transfigured, minds awakened. No mice miraculously restored by the plasma of humans—

No lynx, no leopard, no red roan cow saving herself, using head and hooves to break out of the slaughterhouse—

No rebellious monkeys liberating koalas and reindeer—camels, corn snakes, giraffes, hyenas—no zebras; no flamingos flying home; no Komodo dragon—

If you look out your window tonight, you might see a quick coyote carrying silky children into the world—

Even now in your yards and fields, mice and voles are digging convoluted tunnels, mazes too intricate for any human to follow—

In the printed lines of the story, you will find no lost twin, no drowned child, no requiem shark, no father diving deep, salvaging what he can from this unfathomable ocean—

There is no future where I dive with him, lanternfish lighting our way. We are not afraid of electric rays, angel sharks, wolf eels. We love sinking down, becoming other—

With photophores bright as eyes, lost children watch over us—

The past shall remain dark: you will never see my father's sister, one leg gone at the thigh, infection deep in the bone, bacteria spilling into blood, sepsis—

Rain streaks the window. Nothing my father has to give— no blood, no bone, no birdsong, no river of love can save her—

The copper skins of madronas peel away to expose wet green flesh beneath them—

In breaking light, into a sky vast and muted, pink and lavender, the white gull flies high, catching light, becoming light, a point of light between clouds vanishing—

You will be offered no intimations of the mycorrhizal mind beneath the forest. Trust me: you will not be obliged to imagine a human form dissolving, a child unborn, feeding stars, feeding microbes—

Love comes as rain and fog, the cries of crows, their soft laughter—

In the utter confabulation of my life, there is no light-bedazzled boy zipping between cars, flying on his skateboard—no scarred man lying in a bed in his sister's house, unremembering—

No snow, no camellias, no hands in the dirt, no tulips—

In their elegant simplicity, the transcribers of these parables believe time moves at one speed in one direction. They have no knowledge of prodigal children becoming light, streaking backward through time, returning to their parents—

The dangerous boy who steals a Glock pistol from his neighbor appears. He shoots rabbits and birds; a white porcupine; another child—

On the nightly news there is no time to mention Ray or Polina—

No water pistol, no fleece robe, no smoke, no open window—no feral dogs, no laughing girls crushing a stuttering boy, cracking a boy's ribs under the bleachers—

No story you read or hear includes the possibility of compassion between a runaway girl and the terrified boy who left her in the forest—

You will not feel fog—

No matter how many stories you read, you will not imagine Jude Whitaker no longer a boy, three years older: long limbs, strong shoulders; hips lean, core muscled—

Jude, released from juvenile prison, driving Polina's truck, living with his mother—working for a farmer, dressed as a beekeeper: white mesh suit, white gloves; white hood, thin veil—

No longer reckless, Jude Whitaker is learning to build hives, find wild swarms, trust bees, gather honey, remove parasites, use a smoker—

He is learning to move as the sixty-two-year-old farmer moves, graceful as a dancer—

The smoke from burning fabric made of jute calms the bees, calms the keeper—

Jude and the farmer plant flowers to tempt bees: snapdragon, foxglove, lavender, yarrow. They let dandelions flourish and go to seed, parachute and proliferate—

At the borders of the farmer's land, cherry, apple, plum trees blossom—

Jude Whitaker is learning to bring forth from the earth—to let the bees and the farmer bring forth what's within him—

On the way home, he remembers to stop at the grocery store so that he can make dinner for himself and his mother: broiled salmon, steamed asparagus, perfectly baked golden potatoes. He washes the dishes by hand. It is good to be clean, good to stay busy—good to clear the mind, to think only of the soap, the plate in the hand, the water—

Alone in his room, brain buzzing, he composes a letter to Orelia, describing the plants bees love, the crops they pollinate—how by keeping bees, he and the farmer might for some brief time be two among many saving the world—

He tells her to stare at the sun as long as possible, then close her eyes tight, press her fists into them—

The kaleidoscope, the numinous explosions of color, are a beginning, a way to imagine what a bee with her thirteen thousand eight hundred lenses sees inside a flower—

For Jude, this bewilderment is another way to undo the self—

He does not ask to be forgiven. He is not waiting. He folds the letter and a stamped envelope into another envelope and addresses this one to David Zaer. In the note to David, he asks him to read the letter and mail it to Orelia if he thinks it might bring peace or delight—if he can be sure these words will not in any way harm her—

In the stories others say are true, there are no bluebirds, no vireos, no flocks of iridescent starlings sucked into the engines of airplanes—no warblers or babblers, no larks, no thrushes—

You will not hear their full-throated effusions, lungs full of fumes, wings flared in fire—

Nor will you be compelled to behold the utter catastrophes of kestrels, killdeer, terns, herons—

No one speaks of a man with a white beard sitting at the water's edge, washing bones, cleaning the world—

And you, my nurse tonight—*my angel, my savior*—so peacefully suctioning my tracheostomy tube, singing our names, *Orelia, Sakina*—you who believe I am here and can hear, you whose voice is an exaltation, the blessing of us, our sanctification—you who come to deliver me from drowning—*my bliss, my tranquility*, you and this night, the way we are now will never appear on the news, in the papers—

Nor will there be mention of you coming another night, singing *Halima, Kione, Natori, Radhi, Jamil, Jana, Malika*— giving to me your mother's and father's names, your brothers, your sister—

I told them about you. They pray for you. Natori says you are my gift. Malika says someday you'll save me—

The transposers of my story do not divine the devotion between a reassembled man and a misaligned girl come back from ever—

Reimagined, resurrected, they know pain and the fear of pain, the consolation of each other—

Their desire to be close to death is inescapable—

contrast dimmed, color unsaturated

Through their own bodies, they know that near death and in the deepest deep of sleep, it might be possible to enter the mind of the unnamable—

They have been ravished, wrecked; returned; ruined—

At low tide in a future unforetold, the girl and the man are making a spiral of smooth white stones, largest to smallest, ovals from the edge of the beach to the edge of the water. If you were here in the particular light of this day, you might begin to perceive the stones not as things, but as interludes, occasions, evanescent beings, shimmering stones flecked violet, gold, green, silver—

Some scintillate more vividly than others—as if in recognition—as if in lives long ago your lives entangled—

You might imagine you see them dissolving, breaking into grains of sand, even now through time dispersing—

Together, without words between them, the man and the girl move stones from noon till twilight, knowing that the waves of the rising tide will undo everything they've made here—

They see the future and the past: suffering mute, pain transient: every body brief and eternal: *ecstasis, poiesis*: thoughts passing through the infinite mind of the infinite cosmos—

Standing dizzy beneath a vast opening of sky, bluest blue of another world, seeing and not seeing the place where blue sky meets blue ocean, they feel the limits of their human selves, the exact grief of human bodies—

Even now, knowing the unspeakable, they look at their hands, hoping to see light, white light passing through them—

If you wonder how we survive, the stories untold offer these answers—

In a dream the boy dreams of himself, he is bare and unafraid, bees covering his pale body—

Sakina, it is true what Malika told you: after a night when you spend all night wearing your face shield and mask,

changing your gloves eighty-three times, suctioning tracheostomy tubes—*first one and then another*—when you dare
not hope to restore but try just to keep alive a child with
skin the color of ash; a paramedic who's lost forty-seven
pounds, a third of his body; a woman pregnant with twins;
a ninety-nine-year-old veteran—

> *vessels inflamed, brains on fire*

All dreaming themselves dead, feeling themselves thrown in
a ditch, buried in a pit with thousands of others—

> *awake, aware, voices murmuring*

Not everyone in the pit understands it is time to stop
speaking—

After this night, *so many nights*, you sit in your hot car, still
wearing a mask, windows rolled tight, an obliteration of
morning light intensifying the heat through the windshield—

You are sick with sun, *stroked*, nauseated—you want to
know how it is, how it feels: this dying, this not breathing—
this delirium, this fever—you no longer remember how to
open the door or crack the window—

And it is now, as Malika promised, I come to save you—

> *I am as you believe I am*
> *as I will be in our future*

Dream or vision or myself in this body, I come with two
liters of cold water. I come to save us from ourselves. In

mime, I show you how to unlock the door; I pull my mask down to mouth the words: *Please, Sakina, we love you.* And you know I mean your mother and father—your brothers and sister—the soon to slip free of time, the miraculously awakened—

You fumble and your hands are thick with heat; your fingers stupid—

But you do lift the lock. Malika and Natori help you—

I pull my mask up; open the door; pull your mask down; step quickly away from you—

You are gasping now, breathing—

And it is hot, still so hot—

And I say, *the trees are not far, Sakina—*

We can walk there; now—

All of us—

We can walk into the forest together—

The 7th Man

✦   ✦

:   :

You can't believe how graceful we are, six men moving as one, each sensing all others—but not watching: the eye need not see the hand to know how the hand moves, to feel what the hand is doing:

We are watching the 7th man, the one between, the heart at the center, the one who brings us here, strange and beautiful: we are dancing the man down the hall, strapping the man to the gurney:

He's not the real man—not Leonard Loy Hayes, not Aureo Montoya—not today, not this hour—not one of the many gone and still to come: no, one of us today:

Mick Delaney, a small man with terrible strength: vein in the neck popping blue, dark vein in the temple throbbing:

That bounce off the ball of the foot—he likes to be the one, moving six men to his rhythm:

Mitchell Dean Delaney, a man we know but pretend not to know—the accused, the condemned—he killed his wife and her mother, dumped three bodies in a ditch, doused a

living man with gasoline, set a man not dead on fire—dese-
crator of human life, human waste to be excreted:

I've walked 131 men down this hall—strapped the chests of
29—left leg, right shoulder—secured the wrists of 40 men:

You learn things about a man, feel the blood running
through him:

Helped to unstrap and lift 131 human bodies: fathers, sons,
brothers, uncles—loved or unloved, claimed, disposable—
gone from this earth: cause of death: legal homicide:

There will be no body today, only Mick with his eyes closed,
Mick strapped tight and still twitching, a man we love—*yes,
love*—but men among men never say this:

Mick says, *I do have some last words—I'll tell you later*—a
joke, *yes,* as if, *later*: Mick, our friend, whose children played
with our children, whose wife whispered with our wives—
in the garden, in the kitchen—she knows secrets about us:

Our fears, our failures—love here is not a useful emotion—
not in the performance, not in the rehearsal, the 7th of 77
times we will follow the steps, observe the protocol:

Till we can do it in our sleep, till we are doing it in our sleep,
again and all night, dreaming ourselves into death:

Over and over:

Till the curtains part and we are gone—unknown, unnamed—actors erased from the stage:

We will not be accused, not held accountable:

Riley goes limp and we have to drag him—95 seconds down
the hall, 67 more to hoist him on the gurney—we need to
be prepared: Riley Ferrell, 187 pounds of resistance—a
mass to be moved—he's swearing like a man about to die,
like a man afraid we'll kill him—words I've never heard him
say—wild conflagrations—all those images burning in my
brain:

Do not turn away, do not be distracted:

I have the left leg, Troy straps the pelvis—Mick presses
hard on the ribs—Everett pulls the chest strap:

Fear now will not stop, remorse here will not save you:

We are breath inside a breath, the 7th man's last gasp, sweat
on skin, heat, our hands here and here, the smell of smoke,
buckles tightening:

The 7th man knows what we've done—*your hands,* who we
are, *on me*—but will not waste his breath to blame:

No, he says crazy things, *I forgive,* or, *you've been kind*—he
says, *thank you:*

The one laid out, the one on the gurney, the soon to be dead
man is already singing, *as long as life endures:*

That voice, *amazing grace,* lower than his speaking voice,
moving into me:

We know this man—we watched him all afternoon—we brought him his dinner—nothing special, not since one man ordered and refused to eat: chicken-fried steak, mashed potatoes: *with every breath*—he dumped and flushed—*I defy you*:

Now they take what we serve—faded peas, bleached bread—something brown resembling meatloaf: we watched him eat: hand to mouth, every mouthful:

We hosed him down, we saw him naked:

He's been singing all day—we made him bend, we watched him open:

We looked inside—he looked just like us:

How sweet the sound, into my ear, touching my eardrum—all day, *my fears relieved*:

His whole body trembled into song—a trombone: wind moving through, lips vibrating:

He tried to teach me—I sputtered and spit: the music impossible:

Left wrist, right ankle, *the sun forbear to shine, but God*, the places we touched—here and here—those hands, those fingers, *forever mine*, my hand on his back as we walked, cell to gurney:

I am forbidden to touch—unless to take down, to subdue or lift, unless to drag, unless necessary:

A man has a choice: a man has his freedom:

Convinced, coerced: he wants to walk like a man: he intends to cooperate, *my hope secures*, die like a man, keep his dignity:

The warden is the 8th man, the eyes of all, watching our spines, *the Lord has promised good to me*, hesitation of the hip, my hands, *I once was lost*, murmur of the heart—*Officer Arnoux*—the warden wakes me:

But the hand that touched can't untouch, *and now am found*, the voice that entered shall not cease:

The 7th man feels it now, the heat of my palm pressed to his back, firm and tender, not to push, but to reassure, to keep him strong, to keep us moving:

Twelve years he's known what only God should know, exactly when:

Now the day has come at last, the hour of dusk, the moment:

The clock on the wall glows green, 6:07:

Minutes now are everything, *the earth shall soon dissolve*, a man doesn't want to go limp, *wives whispering*, doesn't want to lose his legs, wants to sing, pretend he's one of us, pretend we're only practicing:

We are practicing—numbers fizz and hum, time vibrates:

: :

We take turns as the 7th man because no body is the same
and every man responds differently:

Neville Trace, blessing us in his mind—to keep himself
calm, to keep the legs steady—a mountain of a man,
Neville: he could bring us down with one breath, the
chest suddenly huge, arms stretched wide, wings whirling—he could destroy: the mass of a man converting to
energy:

He fills the space between, he fills the gurney:

6:09—we see the pulse of his enormous heart, *here*, beneath
the shirt:

Rivers of blood, the surge of Neville's blood, the blood of a
man this size could drown us:

I love these men as the hand loves the heart, without think-
ing—the body not mine alone, but part of many, the mind
travelling out of itself:

I know where every man is, what each hand is doing:

It is important to forget your friends' names, cries at twilight, children playing, a girl with bloody knees, a boy in the woods, hiding:

It is dangerous to think: memory now will not help you:

We need no philosophers here, *why and why*, no counterfactuals—your mother, your father, and one eye gone:

How did that happen:

Years too late, we need no questions—Sam, Troy, Everett, Riley—no mitigating circumstances: the man doesn't want absolution—your love or rage make no difference—he wants to be a man among men, to walk with you, to sing, to touch, *was blind but now*, to be your companion:

His life depends on you—no mistakes, no fumbling—no opportunity to bolt or flail, no temptation—no pepper spray in the face, no reason to fall and fling, to hurt, to bring you down, to die before he dies:

Your arms could choke, your weight could crush him:

So many things can go wrong—now, and later: the 7th man jabbed again and again—every vein collapsed: all those years pushing drugs into himself, and now the needle spikes the hand, the leg, the neck—*we'll have to cut to hit a vein*:

And the man laid out, strapped tight, soon to depart says: *no, here, let me help you*:

It is dangerous to doubt, to drive away after dark, to think, to remember, to go home, to sit alone in the dark, to pop the light in the kitchen:

   :   **:**

131 men: you can't scare me now: I am always afraid, before
and after:

Any Saturday the brother of a man I killed might see me at
the hardware store, might remember me opening the door
of the witness room—my shape, my shadow on the wall—
might see my hands, now, again, and imagine:

His brother number 29:

And there in the hardware store Daniel McFerrin might
seize a screwdriver from the bin, plunge it deep in my kidney:

Not to kill, not to finish—just to teach me how it was for him,
watching his little brother die—how it hurt: *here and here:*

He pulls the screwdriver out, stabs again: *here:* how it was
following me down the long corridor, through the garden,
past the yellow roses climbing a white trellis: *the smell, you
can't believe, the night air:*

He thrusts again: *God, the roses:*

:   :

It is the 7th day and I am the 7th man—Everett, Mick,
Sam, Riley—Neville, Troy—there's no one else: I wake into
the day and know this:

Muted, the light now through lace curtains—Lidia in the
light, dressed only in light, wrapping the lace curtain around
her—you can't believe how beautiful my wife was:

Thirty-six the day she died, Helen twelve the day she found
her:

I didn't know what to do:

Helen, our youngest: she sat down on the bathroom floor,
closed the bathroom door—and waited:

For the light to change, the day to be done, the birds to be
quiet—waited:

Here, beside her mother—where her mother lay in her own
blood—the nose, the teeth, the arm broken:

An aneurysm burst in the brain:

No one could have known, no one could expect this—flash and blur, a dizzy flutter—*no pain*, the doctor said:

The light dissolved: *massive hemorrhage:*

I slept on the couch because the bed, the sheets—who could sleep there:

The couch is good, the couch is narrow—*very quick, very peaceful*—I burned her chair in the yard, her shoes, her pillow:

Helen, Susana—my girls in the house—there, at the window:

Hands on the glass, mouths open:

Gone before she hit the floor:

Blood in the grout in the floor between tiles—the day, the hour, *gone*—I scrubbed and scoured, dizzy with fumes—I could fall, I could die here—I opened the window wide, but the birds—I didn't want to see, I didn't want to hear them:

Years and years and years after:

And even now, today, and the light, and the curtain, and the shadow on the floor, the way the light moves, the way the curtain flutters:

My daughters grown and gone, their mother dead nine years—and now, again, this morning:

I wake in the house alone—a man has a choice: I can go to work, *die like a man*, or I can stay here, drive to my brother's house, hide in his basement—make the damp room my home, my hole—*life without parole*: solitary confinement:

Stay safe in my cell with myself: no hands in the dark, no voices to touch me: no one to love, no words to remember: *I thought you'd die*:

My mother in the dark: *I thought I'd lost you*:

Not remember: a cool rag on my face—my small self gone and returned: six days hot with fever:

Not remember my father—black grass, the scorched field—a field of bloated cows, legs stiff in the air, the air smoke, the sun choked red behind it:

What could breathe:

One calf alive, ears and tail gone, eyes too swollen to see, charred flesh peeling off her:

The sudden weight of the shotgun: my father giving me the gun:

It's time you learned how to do this:

A free man—I can shower alone—no one to stop, no one to watch me:

Drink coffee with cream—scramble eggs, fry bacon—sop the grease with bread, or go to work hungry:

I can crank the radio in the truck, let vibrations blast through, let voices destroy me:

A free man, it's true—but at 5:00 I'll be in the cell, at 6:06 strapped to the gurney:

Repentance now will not redeem: mercy here not possible:

:   :

All appeals denied: I have no right to know what drugs will pulse into my veins, where and how the state procured them:

The identities of our suppliers cannot be disclosed—you understand, for their protection:

We cannot say who will push the drugs: a wizard behind the wall, paid in cash, no way to find him:

The lines of your IVs snake through a tiny window:

You will not see: he cannot know you:

No pain, we can assure, but if there is you won't remember:

Stabbed again and again—Leonard Loy Hayes: 43 minutes to find a viable vein, 26 to push the drugs—*buried alive, nerves on fire*:

My hand on his back, his voice in my body:

I knew every cell of the heart: I felt each cell erupting:

33 minutes more to complete the procedure:

:   :

5:59—at last, already:

No fumbling now: it is very important to keep the time,
follow the steps, observe the protocol:

The warden comes first: to sense doubt or disdain—frenzy,
terror, a tremor in the voice—to know if a man will choose
to walk or if he'll need to be extracted:

Mr. Arnoux, we'll proceed: are you ready:

Yes, my friends are here: they've come to take me:

No shackles or cuffs: *a man has his freedom:*

I choose to walk like a man, but the left leg's in spasm:

Very quick: this won't hurt, no:

This will kill me:

The sun choked red: black grass crackling:

What could breathe:

My father offering the gun:

It's time you learned how to do this:

These men, my friends: the breath of each man, the heat, the hunger:

We are not to blame: we fulfill our duty:

The air they move keeps me moving:

We can't stop now: the door is open:

The warden close behind, watching the hip, the spine, the sway, the stagger:

Mr. Arnoux, please sit on the gurney:

6:02—blood in the vein, green numbers pulsing:

Lie down on the pillow, please:

The gun kicks hard: the left eye twitches:

I stretch my arms wide on the arms of the gurney:

The blast destroys: the green clock buzzes:

Left leg, right shoulder: Sam has the chest, Mick straps the pelvis:

The wounded calf kneels in black grass: her blind eyes see, her whole heart knows me:

Neville leans into the ribs, Riley cinches hard:

To get the job done, to be sure, to complete this:

Blood spills in the grass, the heart huge, blood pumping:

And my father takes the gun, shoots again, through the head, to be finished:

39 seconds: breath and smoke: my friends vanish:

But their weight is here: shoulder, sacrum, *as long as life endures*, the shape of each hand: leg and belly:

Only the warden now, the warden standing behind, watching the clock and me, counting seconds:

:   :

Two humans wearing masks appear: they look very clean—
one tall, one narrow: blue scrubs, the smell of soap—human beings dressed as nurses:

They do not speak: I cannot know them:

*Please, your names, your faces, let me hear you say, let me see
you:*

They wrap rubber tubes around my arms, wait for veins to
pop, prepare to penetrate my veins, find the perfect place to
open: they swab my arms with alcohol:

So sweet the touch, their touch probing: I have no right to
ask: *how many times have you come to this room: how many
veins like mine have you entered:*

I've walked 131 men down this hall: Willie, I confess: we
walked through the valley of the shadow of death: I hosed
you down: I saw you naked:

Doubt now will not release: hesitation here is not useful:

Due process does not demand that every conceivable step be taken at whatever cost to eliminate the possibility of convicting an innocent person:

Willie Jay McFerrin, twenty-eight years old, IQ 87: he wanted to pray: he asked me to help him: *I fear no evil:*

Who knows if he choked that girl:

Errors of fact discovered after a constitutionally fair trial do not require judicial remedy:

Sophia Stetter, five days gone: Willie found her again or for the first time: half buried in leaves and dirt—dirt in her mouth and eyes: *she smelled so bad, and the dirt in her mouth: I didn't like it:*

Willie Jay dragged her into the woods: tried to stop the smell: covered her with sticks and rags, set the rags and sticks on fire:

Fifteen hours of interrogation: no food, no sleep, no prayers, no lawyer:

My brother Willie was afraid of the dark: he slept with me: he slept with our sisters:

Fifteen hours: the detectives told him the story over and over: how he pummeled and choked: *you wanted to kiss, you wanted to love her:*

And the dusk, the dark, the day done—I was afraid:

The trees, yes: I wanted to burn, I wanted to hide her:

Fifteen hours: until he believed, until he saw his small hands
on her white throat: until Willie Jay McFerrin felt himself
lift and choke and shake and snap her:

Willie: 5-foot-4, 122 pounds:

Sophia Marie: 146, three inches taller:

You tell me how my brother did this:

I didn't go home that night—my wife, my daughters—I
didn't want to see: light from the porch, the limbs of trees,
a tire swing dangling in the dark—and the smell, *my God,*
the roses:

Didn't want to hear: voices from another room, muffled
words, two little girls in their bedroom, laughing:

I drove to my brother's house: I hid in his basement—
scoured and scrubbed my skin—blood in the grout, down
the drain, in the shower:

Holy, holy, holy night:

:   :

I am afraid everywhere: afraid of a woman with bare brown thighs, soft brown belly—I follow her in the grocery store: she feels me close—she knows: skin on skin: *make me whole*: I want to touch her:

No, never: my eyes, my hands: for crimes committed and imagined it is my day to die, the 7th man strapped to the gurney:

My throat burns:

131 men: I heard your last words: your voices entered my skull, *how sweet the sound*: I loved the sound: I go listening for you everywhere:

Just one more thing—please: one drink of water:

The warden refuses this:

We're done here: we're finished:

He removes his glasses—a signal, a sign: permission to the wizard behind the wall, the one who waits, who pushes drugs into the tubes, who does not imagine, who never sees me:

What he offers now flows through tubes, snakes out this window, ignites as it hits the vein:

Pentobarbital will kill a horse: if there's pain, you won't remember:

I do remember: sky scorched red, front legs folding—no air: chest heaving high, eyes not seeing—the girl, the calf, Leonard, Willie—remember as if I saw: Helen in the bathroom, waiting for the light to change, there, on the floor, with her mother:

:   :

My friends return: never in my life have I been so glad to
see them:

Bewildering to feel their hands, to think I might be dead,
my body here, my body conscious:

Merciful to love them, to forgive, to know their hands, to
be so grateful, to hear buckles undone, *my friends*, to feel
leather straps loosen, to lie limp, dead weight, to be dead,
to surrender:

They slide their hands under—Troy, Everett, Riley—lightly
lift, gently move me: one gurney to another—Neville, Sam,
Mick:

I'm alive: the hearts I hear my own, the breaths my breath:
the men I love wheel me out of here:

Silent, holy:

Now we are prepared to kill: now we are ready:

I am the 7th of 7 men: no more rehearsals:

Four nights of peace and then together my friends and I will strap down and sedate, paralyze and poison, stop the heart, end the grief, annihilate the mind of Aureo Montoya:

Please, tell me: where do we go: who do we touch, after:

Father, husband: Aureo Montoya robbed a liquor store, pulled a woman from her car, sped off with her baby—hit an old man in the street—snapped his spine, cracked his femur—left an old man to die:

Ditched the car: ditched the baby:

Two kids, my wife pregnant—no heat at home: a rathole with a roof— the landlord threatening to evict us:

Five hundred could have saved our lives—but as you see that didn't happen:

Aureo Montoya shot and killed a policeman's dog:

She had me by the throat: I thought she'd rip my face off:

All is calm: we will kill this man: very quick, very peaceful:

:   :

And then I was driving home, dusk: almost home: nineteen miles:

I remembered a voice in the bathroom, a face in the mirror—not my face—a face behind—I had no face:

I mean I didn't want to see my face: I was dead—it was crazy:

No one shined a light in my eyes: no one listened for a heartbeat:

I was dead or not dead:

No needles in my veins—no need to remove them: the medical team did not return: even now, they keep their secrets:

Only my friends appeared, weirdly quiet, unwilling to look me in the eyes as they slid their hands, as they cradled my body:

The gurney rolled—lights too loud, lights blazing—my head a hive, fingers buzzing:

Then here we were, safe in the hallway:

Mick gripped my hand and pulled: I remember the body
sitting tall, the body straight on the gurney: I felt my feet hit
the floor—here I was—I was standing:

Alive as Lazarus, someone said, voice bouncing wall to wall,
rib to rib inside me:

Alive to die again, not knowing when or why the next time:

Then the face, a blur, Mick behind me in the bathroom: *grab
a beer,* he must have said: and something like my voice said,
not tonight, catch you later:

I remember splashing water on my face, feeling my face with
my hands, water flowing between fingers:

In the car, the smell: piss and blood, an open wound, the
mouth infected—shit smeared, blood spilled—the skull
slammed into a wall, the weeping wall, the body open:

2,329 human beings, all these men, human waste kept in
cages: the walls and floor concrete, concrete permeable: you
can't scrub, can't scour, can't bleach the skin—the smell inside and out—skin of the naked self, the self permeable:

*It's true: I did these things—robbed, choked, hit, killed—yes, I
shot the dog: but I never hurt the baby:*

The men in the car, with me, the smell everywhere:

Aureo Montoya: six years in prison and free to work on the
prison farm:

A slave in the sun: and there I was, and there he was, and the stick I'd found was sharp, and the sun in my eyes, and the stick in my hand, and he was close and hot, hotter than the day, and the light, and I must have stabbed him in the throat: the stick was in the throat, in the vein, and I pulled it out, and the blood, and then I was in the dirt, pinned down on my face, two guards grinding me to the ground, and he kept spurting blood, dying in the dirt, dying right beside me:

What you say must be true:

As long as I'm alive, nobody is safe here:

I rolled the windows down, let the cold take me:

What he did to me I won't confess: when I'm dead three days, I'll come back and tell you:

:   :

So slow, swerving to the side of the road—letting wind blow, letting gravel jolt me—pulling back into my lane, every car surging past, every human being passing:

Orange flare of a cigarette, a man alone, smoke and dust: my father alive, but moving fast: a woman with a little dog in her lap, the dog's dark head out the window:

A husband and wife leaning apart—something said or unsaid—not yet and maybe never:

Please: children crushed in the backseat, four or five— everyone undone—climbing over and back, one side to another:

Forgive him now: you never know what will happen:

I saw houses full of light, bodies moving behind curtains— breath and smoke: broken teeth, brains on fire—jack-o'- lanterns grinning from the steps:

Faces torn, skulls empty: a church with a neon cross:

Light of the Redeemer: two bars flashing their names: *Last Chance, Merle's Refuge*:

Blisters of light between trees: shacks along a winding path: a house alone, an open field:

Something had happened here, but no one knew—they couldn't see it—or it was happening now, coming into being this very moment: a shadow crossing the earth—clouds hiding the moon—nothing more: dust and smoke, clouds and field, forests of oak and pine: the world at dusk, driving through it:

But the shape had life and form—a herd of cattle moving as one, as if in flight, as if fire—*no*:

Too fast, too quiet—the shadow becoming deer, a wave of living beings, not yet bedded down, awake and alive, suddenly startled: watched from the woods by a cougar gone astray, or the bobcat who lives here:

And then they too were behind, and it was impossible to know, now or ever, and the rumble strip bounced me back into my lane:

Almost home: 16 miles:

：　　　：

No light spilling from the porch, no swing, no voices—no
reason to be afraid, no shadows behind curtains:

The couch is good, the couch is narrow: you can stand in the
shower all night: let water scald, let water numb you:

And then I saw them: a family in another car, not passing—
traveling along beside, moving with me:

A man and a girl in the front seat, a baby in back, strapped
in a car seat: a man and his child bride, or a man and his
daughter—the baby her son, the baby her brother—I wanted to know:

The answer to this seemed very important:

Voices in the car blurred—I swear I could hear: too many
voices at once, the man arguing with himself—repeating,
rewinding—too many words, words overlapping—and
then something else:

The girl playing piano in her mind, hearing each note—call
and response—each note pulsing through us:

Reverberation in the throat and diaphragm—alto, sopra-no—Lidia and her sister Florence: they could both sing either line—my wife, her echo:

And I knew before I knew—the stuttering heart, breath catching: the stagger when you start to fall—blood in the brain—the sudden weight of the self, the snap of bone, bone cracking:

And even now, the girl in the car playing piano that way—two melodies at once, breaking into separate tempos:

A sparrow singing two songs:

How could she:

And still the car did not pass, but the music faded—wind, pines, distant fire—the man's argument swelled, the baby whimpered:

The girl unbuckled her belt, turned, leaned over the seat—touched the baby's face—her hands, her fingers—my face: *shush, almost home*:

Almost home, 14 miles:

Voices stabbed the man's skull—jolts of light, vessels burst-ing—adrenaline shooting down the spine:

Gone, the car sped down a hill, around a curve: *shush*, the soft voice, the piano, the baby's cry, the man's curses—gone: but the heart hurt—no air, lungs heaving: I gripped the wheel hard, to stay on the road, to stay steady:

Then the road straight, but so many lights the lights blurred and I didn't know the girl's light from any other:

A rise and dip in the road—everyone gone—only the dark, the shapes of trees, deeper darkness—*no one, nothing*—my lights too dim:

I can't find you:

Then too much all at once, flares of white light—everything wrong—cars jumping lanes—light blasting:

Nowhere to go but over and down—rolling now, down the gully:

:   :

Blood rushed to my head: it took some time to think, to reason—my head hurt, my head too heavy:

Gasoline leaking in the grass, sparks flickering from the engine:

My body dangling upside down—I would die strapped in, on fire if I stayed here:

A man alone, hanging from a seat belt:

I tucked my head to my chest, loosened the strap an inch at a time, eased myself down to the roof, kept my head tucked, released the belt and rolled, crawled out the window:

How far could the road be:

But it was far, the rush of cars a distant river, all their lights obscured, no way to know, no lights to follow—no light of stars—only the moon drifting between clouds, illuminating clouds, a ring of gold and orange—showing half its face, disappearing:

Sirens howled, wailed into the night from two directions: rose up through earth, through bone, then faded:

The moon bright and gone, stars unseen, dogs barking:

High and fast and far away—another low and close—a third one growling:

One wild in the woods: the mockingbird mocking:

You are the ones: I thought the dogs would smell me here, find me in the grass—lie down or lead me to the road— howl till humans came, till human voices touched me:

Only the bird continued: becoming a pack of dogs, the opossum hissing—crickets and frogs—the crow, the sparrow—scolding then breaking into song—warbling in its own voice, whimpering like a child:

I wasn't hurt—I could crawl—I could stand—left leg weak but I could walk—I could climb—find a stick to support— get back to the road and wait—or rest; or sleep; or die here:

I heard the first sputtering notes of a trombone: the mockingbird tempting me toward the woods, into the dark, away from the road, and I thought, *no, not here: I saw you die: I killed you*:

But Leonard, I loved that sound: I have been listening for you everywhere:

The shapes of trees seemed kind—leaves rustling in the dark, needles whistling—they knew me—in every hidden ring a year we'd shared: our lives, our secrets:

I stumbled toward the grove, deeper and deeper into it—I was not afraid of the dark—I grabbed limbs as I walked, felt vines of wisteria:

Tupelo and pine, hickory, maple: they remembered me hiding here, that thin, fatherless boy—that quick, quiet child—I loved this damp earth, trees so close they blocked the sun:

I might meet an alligator here, a gray fox climbing a tree—a bat, a skunk, a flying squirrel—crawling deep in the Piney Woods, I might come face to face with a black snake constricting a rat—God, now, imagining the world:

I buried myself in leaves and needles, dead for an hour or a day, a boy so lost in the woods not even light could find me:

And now, again, the moon behind clouds, the clouds beyond trees, the voices of owls:

How sweet the sound:

I must have closed my eyes—but I didn't sleep, I swear: I didn't move, I promise:

:   :

Safe and still, so little difference between breathing and not breathing:

But I did breathe, choked and gasped, a cloud of smoke clotting the lung, dirt in the mouth and eyes—the world becoming smoke and fire:

The air had a voice: throat torn, bowels burning:

I smelled the bodies of trees—not just ash but charred wood—pieces of trees raining down:

I heard the cries of cows all night:

The earth, the sky, the air dissolved:

Nothing breathed: I stood at the window—hands on the glass, mouth open—refused to go outside: *no, never*: denied what I saw:

Backhoes digging a trench, bloated cows dragged and hoisted—a holocaust of cows—dropped in the trench, bodies bursting:

Everything lost: the cows, the field—black grass, charred fences: the house spared by fire but sold:

For *nothing*, my father said: we moved 596 miles east, Marathon to Nacogdoches, rented a house where my father stared at bluebirds and cardinals, hummingbirds with ruby throats:

As if he wanted to kill, as if they had done this:

Everything wrong—the tiny yard, flowering dogwood—no one could explain:

My father working as a janitor at the school where I went to school: he hated leaving the house at dusk, scrubbing all night, scouring toilets, bleaching urinals, erasing equations he could never comprehend, scraping graffiti from stalls, reading our smut, our rage, our ridiculous obscenities—entering our minds night after night, smelling our bodies in the dark—feeling our small hands on the walls, and then our hands as we shoved him in our spit, tripped him to his knees, pushed him face down in our filth, tied him with string, wrapped it round and round till he couldn't move, till we could write the words, our words, in his mind, on his body:

It must have felt like that, night after night, alone with our grit and sweat, laughter in the walls, threats festering:

I never asked: he never spoke of it:

Even when I saw my father starved, my father wasted— when we knew: the esophagus ablated, the cancer florid:

And then one day I was sitting in my classroom, a singular day, a sudden snowstorm, and it was cold where I was by the window, snow hitting the glass, snow melting, snow blowing hard outside, snow whirling:

Thrilled and alive, children trapped here: the teacher reading words: expecting us to spell them:

Abandon, defile, refuge, resuscitate:

Who knows what she said: *abound, ablaze, defy, annihilate:*

I wrote nothing on the page: *refuse, resist, deny, extirpate:*

It was wrong to sit, to be, to wait here: the snow so close, so miraculous—it never snowed like this—in the twelve long years of my life, never: and here I sat, strapped, *bound, ablaze,* shackled:

And I saw him, a shivering man in a ragged coat, hunched against the snow—a thin man with bare hands, hands too big for his shrunken body:

Refute, redeem: why should he be free: *recoil:*

He must have felt my fire—the old man raised his head and turned, stared back at me, took my fury:

I knew that man:

He looked away, pretended not to see, ashamed of himself or me: he must have fallen asleep in the boiler room, must have been curled there all morning, a heap of sticks and rags, my father—must have heard children in the hall-way—shouts, stomping boots—must have waited for us to go, to file into our classrooms—tried to stand but been too tired—slept again and just awakened:

Deny, refuse:

There was no one to hate but myself, no way to go home and confess, no words to explain, after:

No way to look at the face across the table, to hear my father chew and try to swallow, to see him choke and gag and spit in the sink—this horrible old man, forty-four years old:

The soon to be dead shall receive no pleasure:

Now here I was, older than my father: mouth full of dirt, too weak to walk, half buried: the mockingbird pretend-ing to be an owl, the smell of smoke years gone, my hands numb, the grass slippery:

My brother and I dug a hole for our father: I lay down in that hole, stared at stars, tried to imagine:

Early June, already sizzling:

I slept in the earth:

I woke hot in the dirt, and that day we buried our father:

:   :

We buried my wife:

:   :

We buried our mother:

:   :

Between tall trees, I saw a flicker of light—imagined a
house, a bed, a blanket—a human being with human hands:
someone alive, someone waiting:

Clouds opened: the moon moved between clouds, and I
watched my own hands touch my own body:

The light seemed far but not too far:

The mockingbird's song kept my heart beating:

I crawled between trees, in the dark, in the shadows—
smelled piss and blood—my skin, myself—the body open:

Felt again or for the first time a clot breaking free, the pressure in the chest, my mother kneeling in the garden—lying
down to rest, *here*, suddenly so tired:

My father thirty-two years gone:

And now my mother in the dirt, in the day, with her flowers:

A wave of yellow birds warbling in flight:

I tried to stand: the birds insisted:

My mother alive: minutes or hours:

Three deer watching from the trees:

The songs of birds:

The cool earth, the smell of roses:

And now, today: the deer watching me, leading me out of the trees:

And then: the deer returning at twilight to eat my mother's roses:

:   :

Listen: I crawled out of the forest on my hands and knees:

With the new day and its impossible light falling all around us, I staggered across this broken field:

Now I stand swaying at the side of the road—dirt in my eyes and throat—a man half dead, a man who's been buried—dirt in the shell of the skull, dirt heaped high in the open belly:

Listen: with the bodies of birds trembling into song:

I confess:

I failed to love:

I dragged: I strapped: I killed: I poisoned:

I stopped your hearts:

Over and over:

With the deer quiet in the field, a man too weak to stand— as cars rush by, as wind blows him—is falling to his knees in the gravel at the side of the road, waiting for you—mother, brother, child of a man I killed—waiting, I confess, for you to swerve and stop, sing my name, touch my face, stab to kill, pierce and amaze me:

The Bodies of Birds

⁑   ⁑

The light of late afternoon touching everything—my hands, my face, the wings of birds—illuminating edges of clouds—the kitchen a bottle of light, pale green filling with song—the woman playing piano in a room down the hall—everything clean until the boy, the girl, the husband come home—I'm on my knees in the light scrubbing the floor—my hands glow, cells trembling, body swollen with sound, heart stunned, and suddenly wounded—notes so fast and low they pulse down the hall through the floor rising from me—

I am forbidden to touch the piano—except to dust, unless to polish—but here it is, tremors of light, voices shimmering—she can't stop birds or clouds, light becoming sound, outside coming in, sound becoming body—

My father waits behind hedges at the back of the house—
he's been persuaded not to knock at the door, not to rush or
distract me—I feel him now, hot in the blue Dodge, windows closed, radio throbbing—he's been warned not to let
his music break into the house—those guitars, those voices—my brother Benito's body quivers—tendons struck,
bones buzzing—syncopations jolt his heart—he's hot, he's
hungry—Benito strapped in the back, diaper damp, fist
shoved hard against his teeth to keep from wailing—

                    My father cares nothing
for the woman's peace, her time, the light, her piano, this
hour—he's been severing limbs since dawn, hacking bone,
slicing muscle—nine hours splattered in blood—he hosed
himself down at work, but he carries the smell on his breath,
in his mind, in his hair, on his fingers—everywhere he goes,
the bodies of animals, the chests he cleaved, *God*, his own
chest open, ribs split wide, bowels untangling—he saw
heads in a heap, three men cutting tongues, slabs of tongue
tossed on a table—what he wants now is a dark room, water
so hot it burns, music fierce and fast enough to obliterate
memory—

Bodies waver at the edge of the woods, deer waiting till dusk to float into the woman's yard, strip the roses—those heads, those blossoms—soon to be the flesh of deer, dark dreams of themselves, animals leaping—

Clouds swell, and in this loss of light, shapes become human, men dressed as deer, arms raised above their heads, fingers curved to cast the shadows of antlers— women with glittering eyes, owls carrying children—they ran, they flew—days and years, hundreds of miles—hot wind cracked their skin, their bones broke, their blood congealed— they fell down dead in a ditch, drank dirt and swallowed— they crawled to the Rio Bravo—whirling silt, sweet water— half-humans so thirsty they believed they could drink the river dry and walk—now here they are—they almost made it—

I know them—I see them everywhere—picking jalapeños and pecans, hauling trash, washing windows—I see them mowing lawns, tanks of gasoline strapped to their backs— they spark and spin, burst to flame, explode in your mind, in your yard as you watch them—

I know it is a mistake to call the light tender, but not wrong now to feel its indiscriminate love touching my mouth, the bones of my ears, my heart, my tendons—I remember clouds opened, and the music stopped—the long shadows of pine spread across the lawn—five crows walked between them—I slipped out of the house and into the car, kissed my father's face, pulled my brother's fingers from his mouth—

They wanted none of me, nothing kind, nothing human—and then we were driving home, dusk, almost home, fifteen miles—I turned the radio off, tried to find the woman's music, follow notes down my spine, remember song through my vertebrae—

If it's true what they say—so much space between cells, so much space inside atoms—why can't the spaces of me slip through glass, fast as light, slip through metal—

I know it's possible—a girl stabbed in the heart
doesn't die—a baby dropped five floors doesn't
shatter—somebody wants them to die, but no, they
won't—no, they didn't—

The skin of a sixteen-year-old girl regenerates every twenty-two days—down the throat, through the colon— inside and out, so little difference—continuous, miraculous, my skin protecting even now the open wounds of a burned child—

Weeks or days—soon enough his body will reject mine—but now, tonight, as the drugged boy drifts through dreams he won't remember—*red-winged birds falling from the sky, howling dogs, fur on fire*—tonight, the collagen of my skin fuses into the scraped clean, scoured pits where once there was blood and muscle—

Now we are
one, now we
are quiet—
in the dream
we share I am
unwinding
bandages to
reveal our
spectacular
body, veins
visible, skin
new and fine
as the skin
of a fetus—

You read about us in the paper: *Boy Torched by Bike Thieves*; *Girl Killed in Crash Donates Organs*—thirty-seven days and hundreds of miles between us, but here we are, safe and still, becoming one, the same body—

I surrendered all I knew—heart and lungs, discs of the vertebrae, the dark secret of my spleen, unscarred skin—corneas, pancreas, the delicate bones of my ears, my impossible love, all I had to give— kidneys, liver, veins, cartilage—I offered the gloriously pliable tissue of my thighs, a song moving through the spaces between cells, consciousness unstrung, bowels un- spooled—continuous, miraculous, the bodies I am tonight, uncontained by multitudes—

As a child not so long ago I found the skull of a fox, femur, scapula—skin of a black snake—rib cage of a cat, bones of a bird's wing nested inside it—

I remember the darkening spaces between trees, a murmuration of birds—a funnel, a storm—thousands of bodies
flying as one—starlings swooping low over a fallow field,
black earth cleaved—the smell of dirt, my father's window
open wide, cold wind rushing through us—I remember my
brother's whimper and wailing cry, unbuckling my seat belt
to turn and soothe him—

My father swerved into the left lane
but didn't pass the car beside us—I saw you, a man alone, I
remember how long we stared, some kind of terrible recognition, dark birds whirling between us—my father said, *let
him cry, buckle your belt, leave him*—

I was afraid of my father—spatters of blood on his boots, pigs crying in a kill pit—their flesh, their fat, their long bodies—their miraculous minds—afraid to imagine soft ears, curled tails—pink skin and sweet mouths—their curious gazes, before and after—

Shush, it's okay, we're okay, almost home now—

Afraid to disobey, yes, but I did not turn from you or my brother—*shush, Benito, no*—my brother sobbed so hard my chest hurt, and you read my lips, or heard me—

Impossible I know, but I still believe you saw everything inside: you knew us as dusk became dark, as birds vanished—my father hit the gas hard—angry with you or me or the baby or the pig— the birds, the field, the smell of dirt, the dead, the shadows between trees—you fell far behind, and I thought, *there, it's done, I've lost you*—

Benito only sputtered now, too tired to wail, and I did begin to turn in time to see blue light fill the car—but not in time to sit, pull the strap tight, snap the buckle—

You see us on the nightly news—seven-car crash caused by two girls cranked on Benzedrine, numb with tequila—wind whipping their hair, half sisters in flight, a game of Truth or Dare, the silver Lexus stolen from their father—howling into the wind, runaway children blasting down the wrong side of the road, 80 miles per hour—

You know me, the one lifted in a helicopter—alive, *yes*, but extremely critical—meaning my head slammed into the roof before my body flew into the windshield, meaning ejected as the car rolled, flung into the ditch as the door popped open—

Anika Vela—the name unspoken pending notification of relatives—my mother and three sisters, my cousins, my uncle—my blind grandmother who swam the Rio Bravo with my father no bigger than Benito clinging to her back, who saw her own sister swept away, swirling down the murky river—my grandmother who had to choose sister or son, who swam hard to the other shore, who let her go, who did rescue—Marielena who chose my father and me, the beating heart against her skin, the ones unborn, the lives imagined—

No, not Anika, not possible—

Marielena didn't survive for this, to bury me before her—

You won't see them on the news—my mother, my father—
in a small room with one window where they have been
told, where a doctor has carefully articulated the damage
to the skull, the brain, the stem, the cortex—where he has
explained the fixed eye, dilation of the pupil, the ventilator they use to keep the body oxygenated, the medications
without which my blood pressure will plunge, my heart
stutter and fail—

                                        Now the man is gone and God
here is my father's reflection in dark glass—one terrible
blind eye, the face dissolved—he is pounding his head on
the glass and it hurts or it must hurt, but he can't stop—

As a child my mother prayed to see the face of God—now,
face to face, Tereza Vela turns the light off—

The sun will rise and go down, the flesh be cleaved, the body opened—human hands will hold the human heart—the lungs, the liver—meteors will pummel the earth, cold rain pound the desert—the body of one will be many—ditches will flood and spill, rivers rise and roil—some of the bodies will swirl in silt—some gasp and breathe and swim harder—

And my father will lie
in the dark, listening
to blood, listening to water—
hearing the heart, the rain,
the stem, the cortex—
Mateo Vela will go out
in the light to hold the rib,
to touch the sacrum—
to be one, to be nothing—
to disappear
with the disappeared—
breath and dirt, skin
of the snake, skull
of the rabbit—

There are things you see but can't believe—flames in the street, flames whirling toward your house in the shape of a child—

((*and a woman wearing a mask is stitching the cornea to your eye with sutures finer than the hair of a baby*))

You are wrapping the burning boy in a blanket, pulling the hose straight to spray the body with water—

((*and a man dressed as a doctor is slipping bones in your ear, a kidney in your pelvis*))

You hear howling dogs and you open your eyes in the dark to see what you don't see—birds falling from the sky, your burned hand, the scorched blanket—

Sometimes you are afraid of the heart, the vagus nerve cut, the heart beating too fast always—last summer, waiting for the heart, you almost died of a bee sting—in January, the flu—in March, pneumonia—your lungs filled, your kidneys failed—you died and returned—your swollen, failing heart fluttering inside you—

((*and the woman wearing a mask whispers a needle into your vein: shush, it's okay, we're okay, almost home now*))

You are asleep and awake, fully conscious, eyes closed but able to see through closed eyelids, and a girl with long dark hair is opening your body with the sharp blades of her hands—the one whose face you never dared imagine is singing her way through your bones, speaking your name to the dark as she sews the bodies of trembling birds into your trembling body—

acknowledgments

I thank the John Simon Guggenheim Memorial Foundation for support of this project. I am also grateful to the Lannan Foundation for providing sanctuary in Marfa, Texas, an experience that continues to inform my life and work.

For their extraordinary contributions to research; their playful, healing presence; their imperishable love and unwavering belief, I thank my brothers and sisters. Dear Gary, Glenna, Laurie, Mary, Wendy, and Tom: the ever more astonishing beauty of your lives is and always has been the light behind and within, spilling through all stories.

I thank Caryl Phillips, Valerie Sayers, Katharine Coles, and Michael Martone for decades of camaraderie; for their remarkable, loving, creative lives; and for their generous letters of support and abiding faith when this project was only an idea.

By the companionship, love, insight, and inspiration of my dear friends, fellow travelers, and early readers—Lance and Andi Olsen, Scott Black, Michael Mejia, Paisley Rekdal,